SWEET SUMMER NIGHTS

ANNE KEMP

Sweet Summer Nights

A Sweet Romantic Comedy

Anne Kemp

Contents

For my husband, who sits and listens to me ramble about my books, the characters and their antics, and who supports me always.
You are everything. xx

Chapter One

Freya

I had somehow managed to plan the worst surprise ever in the history of planning surprises.

My family has always gotten together every year around the Fourth of July—it was like our unofficial family reunion time. In years past, we'd all head back to my grandmother's house tucked on the banks of Lake Lorelei, an idyllic piece of Americana nestled in the foothills of Blue Ridge Mountains in North Carolina. When she passed away, I was under the impression we'd continue the tradition, but it seems my family had made other plans this year.

Plans that didn't involve coming here for the holiday.

My favorite holiday, too, I might add.

Standing in my grandmother's home, which now belongs to my Aunt Maisey, I can hear my best friend, Wyatt, now. In one of his last text messages, he told me I shouldn't surprise them—it's like he knew. Of course, he was also the voice of reason who warned me not to move in with my ex, Brad, much the same way he had told me my love for Justin Timberlake would one day wane (I hate when Wyatt's right). But he'd know my family's day-to-day routine better than I would, I suspect. Wyatt stayed here in Lake Lorelei while I went off to school years ago and moved to New York City, so he's actually spent more time with my family in person than I have since then. How weird is that?

Anyway, here I am standing in the middle of my grand-mother's empty five-bedroom farmhouse. I can't be upset no one's around, since it was a surprise from my end. Just miffed. When I call Mom, she apologizes profusely, promising she and my dad will make it up to me.

"You don't have to do that. When you guys asked if I was coming this year, I said no because of work. I didn't even know I'd be able to come until a week ago. Who'd have thought I'd get a new job and have some time off in between gigs?"

"We'll have plenty to celebrate when we do see you." My mother's voice is lilting with pride, sprinkled with her gorgeous Southern accent. I had forgotten how she sounded when she was happy. "I still can't believe I'm actually having fun hopping from state to state with your father in an RV."

She and Aunt Maisey have been through a lot, in fact we all have. My Gran, their mom, passed away a few years ago after a long struggle with Alzheimer's. So if my parents wanted to climb into an RV (a tin can on wheels the way I see it) and drive across the country, who am I to argue? The fact my mom was loving it was a bonus.

"Oh sweetie," she continues, "don't forget, make sure to see Wyatt while you're in town. He always asks about you every time we see him. In fact, the last time we saw him we were at The Red Bird having lunch."

My parents are fans of Wyatt, with my mom always making sure to tell me how he was asking about me, like now. I can't help but roll my eyes hard when she does, and not because I don't like Wyatt. In fact, it's the opposite. Well, at least it was. But now we're friends, and we can't have it any other way.

You see, when we were teenagers, he tried to kiss me one summer, and I ended up with stitches in my cheek.

We were sixteen, and I had gotten my driver's license. I picked him up from his grandmother's house, and we drove around the lake. Wyatt was such an instigator; he kept trying to make me go faster than I wanted to, but I was firm in my choice not to go more than the speed limit. Wyatt, on the other hand, hung out the window and did dumb things that teenage boys did to make me laugh, while I yelled at him to get back inside before he lost a limb.

I was so mad at him in the end, that I did pull over. We sat in the car, arguing behind the dashboard at sunset while watching the sun go down—me telling him he was being insane, and him telling me I needed to relax and live a little. Well, one thing led to another; there was tickling and a moment where we got close...like, really close. I turned away to start the car at the very moment he leaned in for a kiss.

I wish I could say we had "that" kiss, when your lips meet and sparks fly. Sadly, the only sparks we saw were the ones that came from his braces as they scraped across my right cheek. I can still feel the metal of that bracket as it ripped into the soft skin of my cheek. Makes my stomach turn every time. We ended up calling my parents from the local hospital, where I had to get stitches. Now, you'd never even know it had happened; I was young and my skin healed quickly. Thanks to that *and* the dermatologist I found in New York who introduced me to laser treatments.

Ahhh, memories.

Bless his heart, Wyatt never brought that moment up

again. Because of that, and probably because it was simply so awkward, I made the decision to go back to our version of normal. Funny enough, I didn't think he was into me after that and chalked it up to being so close you get your wires crossed. A few months after that happened, he was dating someone anyway. Only thing was, for me, the line had been crossed and my teenage ache for him was real...but hey, I was a kid, it was going to go away, right?

"Speaking of the Red Bird, I'm working there today, so I need to go soon..."

"When do you need to tell your landlord if you're moving?" Mom interrupts, and smoothly I might add. If I could smell expectation, it would be quite pungent right about now.

This is part of the reason why I'm actually okay with the fact it's turned out there's no big get-together this year. Life has been hectic for me lately. I'm about to start this new job as a community manager for a new online social media site, and the best part? I can work anywhere I want to. I don't need to stay in New York City and pay insane rent if I don't need to because I'll be working remotely. The job doesn't start for another six weeks which gives me time to figure out where I want to live—and it's the reason why I was able to sneak in this mini-vacation and come home.

"I'm month-to-month with my apartment now, so as long as I give him a month's notice I'll get my deposit back, don't worry." I knew what she was really asking. She was asking if I was going to come home, but without asking. Very parent-like of her. "And I need to go now, Mom. Maisey is expecting me soon."

"Fine, fine, I won't ask you if you're moving home since I can tell you don't want to talk about it. Just know we'd be thrilled to have you living so close to us again." She sighs playfully on the other end. "We love you, Freya. Give Maisey our love, too."

I disconnect the call and grab my suitcase. I love that woman to pieces, but I really can't talk to her any longer. Maisey has me scheduled to work this week, and I can't let her down and be late for my first shift back. The Red Bird is Aunt Maisey's cafe now, but it used to be Gran's. I worked there every summer until I moved away, and Wyatt did, too. Our grandmothers were good friends, so we've had the privilege of knowing each other since before we were in school. Lucky guy.

Climbing the staircase to the second floor, I can't stop thinking about Wyatt now after talking to my mom. Back when he made his move on me, I was forced to admit to myself that I liked Wyatt, but I kept waiting for those feelings to go away.

You know the feelings—the flutter you get in your stomach when you hear their name or think of the person you're crushing on? The feelings you think will perish and go far, far away as you move on, and even move out of the same town where you both reside? *Those* feelings. They did fade away for me, somewhat. Well, that's not true. I stuffed them down. So far down I'll need one of those super-extendable ladders, like they have on fire trucks, to get those feelings out again. My reasoning is that good friends are hard to find, and I'd rather deal with things my way than to not have him in my life.

All in all, I'm lucky we stayed so close. Well, except for this last year when my job as marketing assistant got a bit more hectic. We've barely connected. Wyatt's landed a new job that's keeping him busy. I'm still not sure what it is; he keeps saying it's a surprise.

I make my way to one of the guest bedrooms upstairs—

the one I'm picking has its own balcony and the best view of the lake. It's also always been my favorite room.

When I walk into the room, I find a note from Maisey on the bed. Of course she knew which room I'd pick. She's known me for twenty-eight years and is one person who can read me like a book.

Welcome, Freya...your first lunch shift in eons will be today! Can't wait to see you and give you a big hug. There's a new uniform here for you, figured you've grown out of your old one. Car is in the garage, keys are on the counter in the kitchen. See you soon. X

Glancing around, I spy the shirt with my name embroidered on the front and grin: The Red Bird Cafe's uniforms are a T-shirt, jeans, and your best pair of Converse. A far cry from my usual dress and heels I'd rock at the office. I change, run downstairs to grab the car keys, and go. If I don't leave now, I'm going to be late. And that's not good.

I go to the counter for the keys, only—there are no keys. There are no keys on the counter, nor anywhere near the counter. No. Where. I grab my phone and text Maisey. She pings back quickly, promising she left them on the counter. I start to text her back, but another beep signals another response from her, telling me to leave her alone. The cafe is getting busy.

"It's not like I asked for this," I hiss into the receiver as if she can hear me on the other end. Okay, I'm a problem solver, right? I can call a cab, but it's a few days before a holiday weekend in Lake Lorelei. Cabs will be busy and fares are higher. I may be an adult, technically, but I'm still on a beer pong budget, sooo... I snap my fingers. I've got it. If memory serves, there should be a bicycle in the garage I can use.

I take off running so fast I slip on the hardwood floor

going around the counter. Recovering, I continue at a slower clip to the garage where I find a bike, alright.

With a flat tire.

Rolling my eyes, I check my watch and my stomach sinks. I always allow myself a window of fifteen minutes before anything I do in case of a minor crisis, crazy traffic, or the urge to grab a coffee before said appointment kicks in. In this case, that window was almost closed. I need to move —fast.

That's when I spy a familiar bright green beacon in the back of the garage. A John Deere lawn mower sits in the corner with the keys already in the ignition. They call to me. No, beckon. If the keys could speak they'd say, "Freya, come and turn us on. Use us. Aladdin, we are your carpet."

I'll do what I have to do, even if I'm not proud of it...this is exactly what my inner monologue sounds like as I climb on board and turn the key in the ignition, ready to steer that stinking lawnmower all five miles into the township of Lake Lorelei proper to work my lunch shift.

Chapter Two

Freya

"I need three iced chocolates and an iced coffee, two lattes, one of them is non-dairy substitute almond milk, and an iced tea with lemon on the side."

Standing at the entry to the kitchen, I'm surprised to find solace in the cadence of my order. The Red Bird is located on the first floor of one of the oldest and most beautiful buildings in town—it's also on the local historical register thanks to the work and due diligence of Gran.

It's all familiar to me—the sounds, the smells. I've spent so many summers right here in this very restaurant helping Gran and then Aunt Maisey as they worked to keep the good people of Lake Lorelei fed and caffeinated. It feels nostalgic, heartwarming, and bittersweet all wrapped up into one ball of emotion.

The cafe is busy today, lively ever, and awash in sunlight with arced golden rays reflecting off the chrome and stainless steel appliances. The brick walls and muted interior add a historical feel for our customers, or guests as Aunt Maisey likes to call them. Her motto? "They're guests in my cafe, so I'm going to treat them like family."

Well, I hope she likes her family super picky and pedantic, because that's who's sitting at table eight. "The faster you can get that order ready, the better. They said they want it yesterday, and they weren't being funny."

"Got it, I'll hurry it up." Maisey is expertly manning the barista station and is brewing coffee for the drinks, her sandy blonde hair pulled up in a high ponytail on the top of her head. "Oh, by the way, there's a sandwich in the window for table ten. Can you drop it off?"

"Of course I can drop off food to that man you keep checking out. Although if you did it yourself, you could ask him over to the house. He could watch fireworks with you on the dock, you know."

I can feel Maisey boring a hole in my back as I flit away to restock napkins. I know she won't dare try to come back at me with customers sitting at the counter privy to everything we are saying. Does she think I'm dumb? I noticed the group she seated at table ten, and I noticed a certain cafe owner get anxious as soon as they sat down. My aunt is normally not the kind of person who worries about her appearance, she's gorgeous no matter what, but today she's rocking mascara and lipstick. My money's on the handsome—strike that, hot—blue-eyed fireman who, from across the room, has been sneaking glances at Maisey himself.

I walk back over to the drink station with a tray and gather the order together, while dodging Maisey, who is in a giddy mood and play-smacking my arm as she leans in, whispering in my ear conspiratorially, "You shush, girl. I just like to flirt, okay, and Jack's some pretty sweet eye candy. Sue me."

"You want him to put out your fire?" I wiggle my eyebrows, knowing it looks weird and, bonus points, it made her nuts. "Is it a four-alarm rager or a couple of love logs sitting on a fire?"

"Stop that, keep those little caterpillars above your eyes under control. I don't need anyone to put out any kind of fire." She cocks her head to one side and stares in the distance. "And I'm going to ignore the fact you said love logs. That's just weird."

I balance the tray and begin walking backwards out of the kitchen, looking Maisey square in the eye, taunting her. Yet another joy of being so close to your family—you know how to poke the bear. "Maisey and Jack sitting in a tree... k-i-s-s—"

Mid-sentence, I slam into what feels like a brick wall with such force that the wind is knocked right out of me. The tray is in a precarious position and starting to do this toppling, teetering thing in my hands. A back and forth wobble, if you will, with me trying to center its balance and prevent every glass and plate of food from being off like a slingshot into various directions around the kitchen and dining room.

To top it all off? I think my deodorant's stopped working.

I watch whipped cream, from one of the iced coffee drinks, plop onto the tray, and the brick wall grows arms—really nice firm, muscular arms at that. But I cannot concentrate on that right now. Honestly, I have no idea who this is behind me, but they are helping me stabilize this drama, and I need the assistance. Now both arms reach around me, my mystery hero hugging me close to his (hard) body so the tray stops rocking as he holds firm in his stance.

I find myself on steadier feet, and the tray calms down. I mumble a thank you over my shoulder and bolt with the order. I want to come back and thank Arms McGee properly. I thread my way quickly through the dining area, dropping off drinks and food, including the crab cake club sandwich to Maisey's fire daddy crush at table ten. As soon as I'm done, I make my way back to the counter to find my hero.

The only two people I find when I go back are Pastor Michael Shannon and his super sweet wife, Patricia—Maisey's regulars who sit at the counter for lunch at least four days a week. I say hello as I peek through the kitchen door, where I find my aunt leaning against a wall chatting with someone who has their back to me. Seeing me, she waves me over.

"Freya, come here, I've got a surprise for you."

I push the swinging door open, smoothing down my hair as I make my way over to them. You know, just in case the mystery man turns out to be some absolute hottie, but I digress. I see him in front of me and wow...the curves of his biceps blend flawlessly into broad, muscular shoulders. I can't help but imagine running my fingertips along the skin on the back of his tanned arms, and it makes me shudder.

Nonetheless, Maisey has a surprise for me.

"Well, I do love a good surprise..."

Maisey takes the mystery guy by the shoulders and turns him around.

Holy cow.

Wyatt?

"Hey, Freya."

The surge of familiarity, nostalgia, and homegrown happiness is instantaneous. It's my Wyatt. Wyatt Hogan. Seeing him brings a flood of memories filled with chasing fireflies under the moonlit sky, skinned knees from falling off our bikes on dirt roads, and summer evenings running through fields playing hide and seek.

Both hands fly to my mouth in an effort to blanket my surprise as he covers the space between us to wrap me in a giant hug.

"Wyatt!!" I honestly can't stop myself. I fling myself into his arms, and we hold on to one another, hugging and laughing for what feels like an eternity.

"Go easy on him, Freya," Maisey teases. "He's a fireman now, so we need him kept safe." Is that pride I detect in my aunt's voice?

"Wait. You're a fireman now?"

Grinning, Wyatt nods. "Guilty. I didn't want to tell you until everything was official. That and it's been a big year of change and a lot of studying."

"He really is a fireman now, although I think Wyatt's technically what's called a probie, right?" Maisey looks at Wyatt for confirmation, which she receives in the form of a nod.

I step back to look at him, pointing to his head. "You got a haircut."

"I figured it was time to lose the man bun." Wyatt's voice drips with sarcasm, but it's sexy on him. "Plus I didn't want it to catch fire."

"Did it really get that long?"

Wyatt shakes his head, laughing out loud and making me laugh with him. I forgot how infectious his laugh could be. "No, but it was long enough. I'm happy to have it short. I can make my shampoo last so much longer now."

"Good to know." I nudge him in the ribs. "You've bulked up! I guess it's for your job?"

"Leave him alone, Freya. He's not just saving kittens in trees all day." She pushes me out of the way playfully as she hands Wyatt his takeout order. "We love our essential workers here, Wyatt, so make sure to remind folks at the

12

firehouse that all of you get seventy-five percent off food at all times, got it?"

Wyatt nods, tipping an invisible hat Maisey's way. "Got it, Maisey, I'll let them know." He lifts the takeout bag. "Everyone's orders are here?"

"You bet. And I made a note on Reid's steak sandwich so Dylan doesn't eat it by mistake again."

"You're the best. Thanks, Maisey." He turns his attention back to me. "And look at you! Honestly, Freya, I had no idea that was even you when I came in. All I saw was someone struggling. Figured Maisey hired a new waitress who couldn't keep up."

I narrow my eyes at him playfully. "So you had to wrap your arms around me?" Not that I was complaining.

"Well, you looked like a sumo wrestler about to fall off a balance beam."

"Really. You're going there? You know, I hold a lot of your secrets, Hogan, don't mess with me. I know where your bodies are buried."

Wyatt runs his fingers through his jet black hair. "You don't scare me, Fredericks. The only time I fear you is when we play darts. Or when you're driving a car, that can be horrific."

"Lucky for you, I'm not doing either at this moment." I reach into my apron pocket, grab the keys to the John Deere, and hold them in the air. "I drove the lawnmower to work today. Someone forgot to leave the car keys—I'm not naming names but we'll say it rhymes with Daisy." Stepping back, I look him up and down. "Gosh, Wyatt, I've not seen you in ages."

"It has been too long, especially if you're being forced to drive lawnmowers." His eyes dance with laughter, while my tummy starts doing tiny flips, back and forth, like a gymnastics team prepping for a meet. Standing in front of Wyatt, I feel a magnetic pull like I've not felt before. Ever.

What is going on?

Honestly, the guy in front of me, who was once a lanky school boy wearing enough braces for his mouth to pass for a railroad, was now a man. He was a man with defined, sculpted arms, tanned smooth skin, and a smile that was as warm and welcoming as it was perfect and charming.

Something was jumbled inside me. I must be confusing things. I mean, I'm back in town and thinking of moving home, and I'm in a place that holds a ton of sentimental value. I must be getting my feelings crossed, right?

Yet, the more Wyatt speaks, the more I find myself not really listening. I can only stare at his lips and think about how amazing it would be if I could stand on my tiptoes and brush my lips across his. Really slowly...

And there it is. That flame I hoped would burn out, the one that lights the torch I carried? I think it's been reignited —it's not just Maisey who's going to need a fire put out.

"Hey, Freya, did you hear me? I need you."

Snapped back to the present, I look around and realize the bustle of the restaurant has intensified. Maisey's seating a new table, giving me an evil glare from across the room, and in the distance the bell starts to ding on repeat in the kitchen, signaling another order is ready and in the window for pick up.

"I'd love to talk more, but it looks like we're about to get busy again." I lean in closer to Wyatt and cross my arms. "You free later today?"

"Hmmm." Wyatt's dark brown eyes sparkle with flecks of gold reflecting the sunlight. "I'm supposed to hit the gym with my friend Dylan, but I'm sure I can postpone it. What are you thinking? Do I need to be free for an adventure? For a meal? A lifetime?"

I laugh as I grab the lunch ticket from the outstretched hand of the line cook and begin loading a tray with the next food order. "We'll start with an adventure, and the other parts can be up for negotiation." I finish placing the last of the plates on the tray before picking it up in one swift, fluid motion and sliding the tray to my shoulder for its delivery. No teetering this time. "Deal?"

"Deal."

I spin on my heel to go, and Wyatt playfully blocks the doorway I need to go through. Seems he doesn't understand it's the lunch rush and I've got hot food to drop off to Lily Donnelly and her book club before they go to the library. Don't want to make them mad. Lily is known to throw her dentures when agitated. "Can a girl get past, please?"

He stands in front of me for another moment, and there's this look on his face. If I'm not mistaken, I just caught Wyatt looking me up and down, as in checking me out and letting his eyes have their way with my body—which would suck for me because I'm sweaty, my hair is pressed into my forehead, and I smell like chicken fingers. We stand off for a moment before he moves to the side and waves his arm out in a chivalrous way as if pointing me forward. "Of course, but the next time there will be a fee."

Okay, that sounded coy. Flirty. I hear the huskiness in Wyatt's tone, and it throws me. It was like his words were G-rated, but the meaning carried an R-rated undertone. I raise my eyes to his, my heart pounding. I'm not sure what to do, and to be honest, all I can hear are my own words all those years ago, when I rationalized it would be better for us to be friends—I'd rather he be my friend forever than an ex-love. Right?

So, I do what's best in the moment for me: I get outta dodge. I give Wyatt my best mini-curtsy before sashaying through the door and beeline it to Lily's table, calling out over my shoulder I'd see him later. As I place everyone's orders in front of them—and move Lily's water glass housing her dentures out of the way—a tingle sneaks its way up my spine.

I feel him watching me.

I turn around to look, and there he is. Standing right where I left him, watching my every move. To top it off, he's doing it with this smile lazily draped across those full lips of his.

A voice inside my head screams at me to not go there.

But I am a very stubborn girl.

Chapter Three

Wyatt

Freya Fredericks is back, and it's about time.

I'm still processing seeing my best friend for the first time in a year when I walk into the firehouse with lunch from the Red Bird. We've both had crazy, intense schedules this past twelve months which didn't allow either one of us any time to catch up, except by text or a quick call here and there to check in. But now here she is, back home. And not only does she look amazing, but she feels amazing, too. It's been a while since I wrapped my arms around anyone, and man if she didn't smell like heaven and sunshine sprinkled with vanilla cupcakes, all mixed together.

"Did you get me a pastrami on rye, Hogan?"

Shaken from my daydream, I reach into the bag, stamped with the familiar red bird logo from our favorite cafe, and toss the small parcel across the lounge area to the person requesting it. "You bet, Jay Dub." He snatches it out of the air and nods his gratitude.

The firehouse is quiet today with a few of our full-time staff taking midday naps in the bunks upstairs. My big news this year is that I became a probie—a probationary fire-fighter—at the Lake Lorelei Fire Department. The firehouse usually has six full-time staff, three part-timers—which includes me—and a rotating roster of local volunteers that vary in numbers depending on the time of year.

This week, though, is always a special case. Lake Lorelei likes to have a week of events around the Fourth of July. Everything is planned with the aim to bring in tourists to our town, which it does and then some. It's a time of year when our population almost doubles in size, at least for a week, so we have more of us scheduled at the fire station than normal.

Scanning the room, I find an empty spot on the couch next to Jay Dub, one of our senior part-timers, who is focused on his pastrami sandwich at the moment. "Man, Maisey's homemade bread is the best. Thanks, Hogan."

"Pleasure's all mine. Does it get me out of parade duty this week?"

"No way, probie." Jack chuckles as he struts into the lounge and joins us. "I'll need you to shine up the fire trucks before you leave today, as well as check equipment and run any checks for safety."

"Got it, Captain. Anything else I can do to help?" Being a probie, I'm well-versed in my daily duties; my running checklist is always a work in progress with the Captain adding to it as needed each shift. I'll admit that some days I feel as if the weight of the station is on my shoulders, but my jobs are important for the overall safety of my team. My goal: to be off probation—and all going well, I'll be promoted to full-time firefighter when my six-month period ends in just a few weeks' time.

"Not right now." Jack tips his head in thanks as he walks out of the room. "By the way, you're doing well, Wyatt. I see you showing up early for your shifts here and introducing yourself around town to tourists and locals. Keep up the good work."

Smug, I wait until the door is closed before spinning to face Dubby, holding my hand palm side up. "You owe me twenty bucks. Pay up."

Dubby chokes on his laughter between bites. "You're holding me to that?"

"You said I'd be gone in the first three months. Got ya, sucker!"

Dubby reaches into his back pocket, pulling his wallet out and then a crisp, new twenty-dollar bill. "Here, don't spend it all in one place...unless you plan on spending it on Maisey's niece. In that case, I'd suggest hitting up the ATM, son, and making sure you can take her to a nice dinner."

"Who? Freya?" Was he nuts? I shake my head. "In your dreams, Dub. She's a good friend."

"Yeah, I know those kinds of friends," the old man says with a growl, wiggling his eyebrows and treating me to an overly expressive wink.

"Freya's different. I've known her since we were little kids." I cock my head to one side, before leaning over and play-punching Dub's arm. "You trying to stir up trouble?"

"Well..." Dub screws up his face. "I happened to stop by the Red Bird to drop off something to Jack. I saw your reunion, and now I'm a witness to the look on her face when she saw you. Trust me, she was not looking at you like you were friend material."

I couldn't have held my laughter in if I had tried. "You couldn't be more wrong. I know that girl, and she has never given me a second look, at least not in that way. Why would she start now?"

Dub stands up and lifts one shoulder, as if shrugging my question away. "You've got a point."

Reaching out for ammo, I grab the closest thing, a newspaper, and wing it at Dub's back as he strolls out of the room chuckling to himself. Only now he's got me thinking.

Was Freya flirting with me?

I've always had this connection with Freya, but to entertain the thought she may be flirting back finally? No way. I shake my head as I polish off my food and make my way out to the main hangar where the trucks are stored. I pinch back a groan. There was so much stainless steel and chrome adorning the two large rigs, all needing to be polished to parade perfection. It's a big job, but it has to be done. It's something we have to take care of on a regular basis to aid in the longevity of the trucks, but the July Fourth parade was *the* day for the trucks to sparkle and shine.

Walking over to the closest cupboard, I reach in and pull out a cleaning box filled to the brim with rags and products for buffing. Experience has now taught me that this is a time when I can find peace in my day and let my mind wander.

And I know exactly what I'm going to think about today.

Freya Fredericks.

If I'm to be honest, I can't remember a time when I didn't have a small crush on that girl. Of course, I talked myself out of it years ago. Freya's friendship is way more important than a stolen kiss on a summer night. Plus, she stone-cold stopped me when I did try, and we ended up at the hospital with her getting stitches. Not the best look for me.

However, today after seeing her, I am questioning that choice.

The Freya I remember had a retainer. She was ridiculously clumsy. She could keep up with me when we raced our bikes, but braking was an issue. If memory serves, she couldn't brake when we were on roller skates either, so the girl has problems stopping. She also has this way about her, where she bites her lower lip when she's thinking. It's a little nuance which I've always thought in the past made her look pretty. Only today when she did it, I didn't think it looked pretty at all. Nope, not one bit. In fact, the word pretty wasn't even on my radar.

It was sexy. She was sexy. Like, the kind of sexy where I wanted to lean in and bite her lip for her...but I can't. It's Freya, and she friend-zoned me so fast that night oh-so-many years ago that I think I'm still recovering from the whiplash.

Thinking back now, I realize I've had it bad for her for years. I thought by hanging out with her all the time, especially during our summer breaks, it would have shown her I was serious or maybe even gotten me a seat at the table, you know? I even went so far as to take a job at her family's cafe so I could work with her every day. When she waited tables, I requested to be her busser so we had the same shift, and Maisey always agreed.

Of course, when I went to kiss her as a young fifteen-year-old (she's a bit older than me, the cougar), and ended up causing her face to be split open...well, that kind of trauma doesn't quickly go away. She had to get stitches, thanks to one of my brackets being pulled off from a Now or Later I was sucking on. Want to talk about being embarrassed? Yeah, explain that one to your friends. I went to see her the next day to talk to her about it, but when I brought it up, she simply held up her hand and stopped me. Gave me some line about how being friends is way more important, so I did what any teenager would do. I gave her a six-pack of Cheerwine and a bouquet of flowers as a get better soon gift and we went back to being ourselves the next day.

Except for the bandage on her right cheek, you'd never have known anything was wrong. As luck would have it, my braces came off as soon as summer was over that year. It didn't matter. I had been shuffled to the spot where good guy friends go to...stay. I'm the friend without benefits.

And because she was the person I liked to hang out with, I wasn't going to do anything but agree. I didn't want to lose her, so I decided then and there, I was going to take what I could get for as long as I could humanly stand it.

I take the shammy and begin polishing the chrome on the front bumper of the big rig. The repetitive motion is soothing, almost hypnotic, and allows me the chance to zone out. I start polishing like it's a mission, but I'm trying to get *her* out of my head. The curves of her waist were perfect, and I can still feel the warmth of her body as she pressed against me. It's marked on my senses and isn't going anywhere, like the subtle scent of her perfume that's managed to embed itself in my shirt.

But I can only see Freya's face in front of me, smiling. Looking at me like she was seeing me differently.

That could not have been my imagination, could it?

"Yo, probie, you hear me?"

I turn and see Jack standing next to me with a weird expression on his face. "Sorry, Cap. What can I do for you?"

Jack has been a mentor to me, and I'm grateful for it. He's had a tough run in life, and Lake Lorelei is lucky we got him to leave Washington D.C. to come run the fire station here. I started at the same time he took the job, so we've had a chance to bond. You know, in the way guys do— we fish, go to baseball games, or eat. Pretty simple, really.

"Was just saying it would be great if you got at least one rig done today, no need to try for any more. I can get the other guys to finish what you don't." He eyes me. "Where's your head? Still at the Red Bird?"

Was I that obvious? "No, sir. My head is straight as a pin, and I'm right here, present and accounted for."

Jack chuckles and pats my shoulder. "Calm down. You're not the first man to see a pretty girl and go all mushy. Just make sure you get your work done, okay?"

"Yes, sir." I turn to give him a mock salute but find he's already gone, like a flash, the same way he came in. I swear, that guy is like a cat. He needs a bell around his neck so we know where he is. Even Jack can see I'm pining for Freya. Freya, whose emerald green eyes can pull me in like I'm the Millenium Falcon and she's the Death Star, but in a less tragic way. Freya, the girl who always makes me laugh. Freya, who was flirting back with me today, and man, did I like it. My body liked it, and so did my heart.

Seeing her today it became apparent—I love Freya Fredericks and always have.

And now she's back, finally, and I heard through the Lake Lorelei rumor mill she might even be coming back for good.

The Fourth of July has always been her favorite part of the year. I know this because I know *her*. And all of my best memories from this holiday are by her side, usually on the dock at her grandmother's house, watching the fireworks explode in the sky above.

If I'm going to get Freya to fall for me, this is the week to make it happen. To let her know I'm still right here and I'm not going anywhere.

This is the week I'm going to win her heart.

Chapter Four

Freya

"Was today everything you remembered?"

Maisey plops down next to me on the end of the dock, handing me a glass of her famous sweet tea. Sweet tea in the south is the best, although some folks make it with so much sugar you can chew it. Oh, who am I kidding? I love drinking those, too.

"It was everything I remembered and more. Who would have thought that slinging cafe hash with your auntie would be so much fun?"

I trace a figure eight on the top of Lake Lorelei's surface with the tips of my toes while turning to Maisey and batting my eyelashes. She's having none of it.

"Hash, girl, that's a 'how dare you' moment around here. Those potatoes are your grandmother's recipe. For your information, she used to grow her own vegetables in her garden and her potatoes used to..."

"...take first place at the county fair." I groaned. "I get it. She was a miracle worker."

"Miracle worker? No, girl, they were just potatoes." Maisey laughs and swats my arm. "I was going to say she was a winner, not try to lay any kind of great prophecy on ya."

"Potatoes or prophecy?" I shrug, deciding to quote our favorite game show. "I'll take potatoes for two hundred dollars, Alex."

"Do potatoes mean Wyatt?"

"Potatoes are potatoes, Maisey." Cutting my eyes in her direction, I watch her take a sip from her glass, making sure she doesn't dare meet my gaze. "It was good to see him. Really good. He's going to stop by later so we can catch up, maybe go out for a bit."

"Ahh, so you're here what, less than two days, and already lining up a date?"

"No, not a date. It's Wyatt. We don't date."

Maisey laughs. No, she actually snorts with laughter that echoes off the lake and reverberates back at us a thousand times over.

"Why is it that you think Wyatt isn't the dating kind? Is it because he doesn't have a lawnmower that's sweet enough for you?"

She has me there. I start giggling, I can't help it. "It was pretty ingenious of me, though, you have to admit it. Not many folks would see a lawnmower and think 'I should drive that to work' but I did. And I got there on time."

"You have a way of making an entrance, that's for sure. For the record, you were five minutes early." She scoots closer to me, leveling her gaze across the lake, taking in the view.

When I was a little girl, this view always made my heart explode. I'd sit up late at night in my room watching the lights from the houses surrounding the lake twinkle on the water, illuminating the lapping waves in a mesmerizing and tranquil way that would always lull me to sleep. Some of those nights, Wyatt was by my side. Sometimes we were in the living room fort we built every year until we were too old for that kind of thing any longer, but we also made sure to spend a few nights each summer in the tent my dad would always put up in the backyard.

Sitting here reminiscing, my lips curl upward. Another memory with Wyatt as my co-star. That boy truly was a part of my life every summer for as long as I can remember.

"That's a dangerous grin." Maisey nudges me in the ribs. "What are you thinking about?"

Against my better judgement, I tell her. "Potatoes," I say with a sigh.

"That's my girl!" she exclaims as she turns in her seat. "I've been waiting for this very moment for years. Wait—as long as potatoes really do mean Wyatt?"

"Maisey, calm down." I laugh. The woman loves love, who can blame her? "I just got back, I'm in the middle of moving home, and I see my old friend who is suddenly really hot and built like a brick wall...what happened?"

"The Lake Lorelei Fire Department, that's what happened." She chuckles as she kicks the water with her feet. "Wyatt decided last year he wanted to join. He had to go through a couple of weeks of workshops to make sure he was fit enough to pass muster. He realized he wasn't as good of form nor as strong as he wanted to be, so he hit the gym harder while taking his classes."

"Well, it paid off," I murmur, rattling the ice cubes in my own glass and thinking back to the skinny, scrawny guy I used to know who could barely manage a pull-up. The instant I think about Wyatt as a fireman, all bulked up and ready to carry me out of a burning building, I shudder with excitement. I wonder what his abs look like? I bet I could grate cheese on them.

For the love of everything, why am I thinking this would be a good idea now?

"He's ripped, and the ladies around here have been noticing him a lot more often, I can tell you that. Good thing you're back to stake your claim."

"Maisey!" I all but spit out my drink. Do I even have a claim to stake? "Look, I've dated Wyatt's friends, not Wyatt. He's the guy who lets me hog the popcorn when we go to the movies, or if we're at dinner and I have food in my teeth, I'm not stressed because it's Wyatt. He's the friend who is always there—he's not the dating type."

I turn to Maisey, certain she will understand now, especially after hearing my sane reasoning. Only I find her biting her lower lip to keep from laughing. I love this woman, but man she can be irritating.

"What? He's my friend. Don't try to make it more than what it is."

"Oh, my poor girl. You don't get it, do you?" Maisey shakes her head from side to side as she leans over and slips her arm around me. "I think it's time I let you in on a secret."

I roll my eyes. So hard it hurt. "What's that?"

"I can see what you don't, and what I see is a boy who has been in love with a girl for years. And the girl? She's so focused on everything else she never saw the boy."

"Now you're making things up. He's never been in love with me. He tried to kiss me, but he was confused. We were young." I groan before continuing. "Lest we forget, I had a crush on Wyatt, I was just quiet about it until I got over it."

"Oh please, like you could ever get over that kind of crush." She hoots and waves her hand, as if dismissing me. "Doesn't matter. That boy showed up even if you were grounded, to watch TV, play board games, or ask your parents if you were allowed to go for a walk."

"He was being my friend, not trying to be my boyfriend." I shake my head, this time with more vigor. Maisey is simply imagining things.

"What about that time when he brought you that ridiculous balloon bouquet?"

It *was* ridiculous. About twenty helium balloons, all in a rainbow of color and three of them were Tweety birds. It was so weird, but it made us laugh really hard. "He did that because I broke up with his friend, Brent, and I was a mess. A sobbing mess and he felt bad. The end."

"Mmm-hmmm. And when Brent tried to get back together?"

I didn't quite get where this was going. "Wyatt wouldn't let me, he knew Brent was seeing someone else, so he told me about it."

"So he was protecting you?"

"He was being a good person." I was exasperated. "He didn't want his friend to be hurt again, that's all."

"But he was always around! Even when you were sick that summer and had to get emergency surgery for your appendix. Who was the one person who found a way to the hospital every day, so he could hang out with you?"

This time, I didn't have a comeback. She was right: he was at the hospital, and then right after, when I was at home recovering, he was here at my grandmother's with me.

Every memory from that time featured Wyatt, that was for sure.

Maisey takes this opportune moment to press her lips closer to my ear. "And you think I'm reading into this?"

"Yes, I do." I jump up and untangle myself from her embrace and shake her words off. I'm already dealing with my own feelings bubbling to the surface, and I know I'm not ready to hear that she or anyone else thinks Wyatt and I are like two ships passing in the night. Especially not after feeling the electrical current go through him and slam straight into me earlier today. I can't control the shudder that envelopes my body as I think back to when he wrapped his arms around me to help steady the tray. There's an appeal to that man, and my body is responding—in a way that I can't help and don't want to stop.

I look down at my watch and realize I need to get ready, Wyatt is going to be here soon. Even though Maisey has me thinking about him completely differently than I have in ages, I need to pack this bag, zip *and* lock it, and put it away now. "It's a shame we don't have time to discuss my love life, or lack of one, any further." Yes, my voice oozes sarcasm. "Wyatt is going to be here in about an hour to hang out."

Maisey shrugs and sighs, turning around in her seat away from me to face the lake once more. "You'd better get a move on and get your butt up to the house and shower. You smell like tuna melts and french fries."

Chapter Five

Wyatt

F reedom.

Being on this back road, racing bikes with Freya is exactly where I want to be. I hear her behind me, choking on the dust coming off my back tires, but laughing. We haven't done this in years, and it feels really good, nostalgic even, to do this with her.

"Keep up, Fredericks!" I yell over my shoulder, standing up on the pedals of the beach cruiser I'm rocking to speed up. Hanging out with Freya could mean so many things, and tonight it meant cruising down back roads in Lake Lorelei, laughing and catching up.

This is exactly what two old friends do. When she suggested we borrow some bikes from her neighbor and go for a ride, I gotta admit it...I was a little excited. I had wanted to turn our night into something with a little more oomph to it. I actually had visions of a romantic bike ride around on country roads when she suggested it, so of course I was all in.

Bottom line? I get to spend time with her. Also, let's

note that I'm the kind of guy who wants to do this with no one ever, but with Freya it makes sense.

I realize Freya hasn't said anything for a few minutes, so I sneak a quick look over my shoulder to see if she's still there. She is, and if I'm not mistaken, I just caught her looking at my butt. I slow down so we're side by side, pedaling almost in sync.

"Like what you see?" Sue me. I had to ask. I'm rewarded when a soft pink flush spreads across her cheeks. I was right.

Freya keeps her eyes focused on the road in front of her. "I have no idea what you mean."

"Come on, Freya. You can't fool me." I speed up, angling my bicycle in front of her so she has a better view. I make sure I'm going fast enough so I can coast on the bike, allowing me time to stand up on the pedals again and give my booty a little shake. "You've got to admit. It's a peach."

Freya snickers. "Mmmm. It's something."

"Would you rather it be more like an apple?" I slow down so I'm beside her again. "Then I can say it's hot like apple pie fresh from the oven?"

"You're hilarious." She laughs again as she speeds up and passes me on her bike, which is not a beach cruiser, I should add. Freya had picked a mountain bike to use, which is a smarter choice for these dirt roads. She's always been a bit competitive, and she obviously wants to take off on her bike and race me. I know this girl. "I'm not a fan of apple pie. I'm more partial to a good strawberry pie, to be honest."

Watching her speed off, I determine I'm not going to be outdone by her, no way. Not by Freya. It's my week to get her to realize she's in love with me—actually, more like get her to understand I'm in love with her—so I also speed up, matching her gait, keeping us next to one another on the narrow road.

"Strawberry pie. Noted. So, is it true that you're moving back?" Too soon to ask? It's all Maisey has been able to talk about the last few months—the possibility of Freya moving home. Only as soon as I ask, I want to take the words back. I hate to admit it, but I'm nervous about what her answer will be.

"It's a strong maybe. I'm still weighing my options." Her voice is coy. "Maisey said I can stay with her for a few months until I find a place, but I don't know yet."

Play it cool, Wyatt. "I'd be happy to have you back." *Where's the cool?* I clear my throat. "I'm sure Maisey will like having you back, too. More than me."

Oh man. I sound...awkward! I try to recover. "Not that I don't want you back, I do, I just know that Maisey is your aunt. So she'll be happy..."

I look over to Freya cracking up. "I know what you mean, dum dum. I'm not sure if I definitely want to be back here, that's the only thing. I've been on my own in NYC for so long, but I want to be with family and familiar things, you know? I love the city, but as soon as I'm here, in Lake Lorelei, I always realize how much of this place has made its way into my soul. It's so peaceful here and simple, even the green in the trees can be more vibrant than the lights of the city—I love it."

"Dylan says the same thing about life here. It's peaceful and simple. That's the kind of thing you take for granted when you live here, I guess." I want to keep her talking as long as I can. Funny enough, I like listening to what she has to say and want to know more. I need to hear more.

She nods in agreement. "Kind of like when we don't know what we have until it's gone. That's how I feel about Lake Lorelei. I didn't understand my appreciation for this place until I went away."

Chapter 5

I feel like she could be talking about us, at least that first part of what she said. You see, I know from my end I didn't realize what I had until she was in New York for good. When her visits home would consist of a quick catch-up during a whirlwind trip, visits that quickly faded away until the times she was coming back were fewer and fewer. Honestly, I had resigned myself to having her be the one who got away, but now we're here and it feels so right to be with her under the evening sky.

I'm feeling buoyed by her mere presence and, in my haste to keep being cool, I decide now's the time to show off a little. Spying what appears to be a hardened berm on the side of the road, I decide to wow Freya with my amateur acrobatic skills and take the bike into a jump.

Now, do I know how to do this? I've seen it done on TV, so I'm sure that counts.

Am I truly skilled enough to pull it off? Well, we'll just have to find out.

Feeling full of myself, I turn and slyly wink at Freya before I pedal off with the nose of my bike pointed straight at the dirt pile. It looks like it's been there for ages, and I can see the hard crusted surface which—in my feeble mind—looks as if it can hold me and the bike. No problem.

Boy am I wrong.

As my front tire connects with the berm, I realize it's softer than it looks. Way softer, like a plush stuffed animal. Or more like a cloud made from quicksand, because as the bike hits the dirt, it also comes to a complete and total halt.

Cue the moment where I flip over the handlebars and fall, without grace, into the ditch. The smelly, stinking ditch. I think I even scream.

I open my eyes, and Freya's there, straddling her bike at the top of the ditch with her mouth hanging open. And wouldn't you know, from this angle her legs look amazing. They're long, smooth, and tanned, and I'm pretty sure they are begging for me to touch them. She hops off her bike and kneels down beside me, balancing herself on the side of the ditch so she won't topple over herself.

"Are you okay?"

I wiggle my fingers and toes. "I think so. But I need to know if that looked as cool as I think it did?"

"Not at all." She's fighting a smile that wants to be exposed, and at my expense, no less. "You looked like a bird that hit a window mid-flight. It was pretty horrific to witness, actually. I should call 911 to help get you out of here?"

I grab her outstretched hand, laughing. "Don't you dare. I know people there."

Freya whips out her cell with her free hand. "Don't test me."

Joking, I jerk on her wrist. It's meant to be a soft and playful move, but somehow things go from bad to worse—and quick.

I tug again, and Freya does a little wobble and loses her balance. I didn't realize how precarious her positioning was until it's way too late. I watch her face change from serene amusement to shock and horror in a matter of milliseconds as her feet slide out from underneath her and she tumbles down, landing square on top of me. Both of us are now lying in this slimy ditch that stinks of rotten eggs, but hey...she *is* on top of me.

To think I was trying for romance.

Freya's face unfortunately lands with a loud thwack on my chest. It's my turn to fight my laughter as she lifts her head to look at me, a giant patch of mud on her right cheek. She's absolutely perfect.

Chapter 5

My turn to check on her. "Are *you* okay?"

She nods, closing her eyes as she sits up on her knees in front of me and rubs her head. I sit up but stop mid-lift when my eyes suddenly come to a rest and focus on her lips. How have I never seen them before? They are full, bowlike and smooth, and the sweetest shade of soft pink I have ever seen.

And I need to kiss them.

I angle myself so I'm sitting upright, and now we're even closer. Her eyes are still closed. This gives me another moment to really look at her—her cheekbones, her skin, and those beautiful lips. I don't even have the energy to stop myself when my hand automatically reaches out to push away some stray pieces of her hair that have fallen across her face.

At the same time I reach out, she opens her eyes and puts her hand up to brush away the same strand of hair, and her hand comes to a rest on mine. We lock eyes, so intensely my stomach thuds and my body shivers. I can feel her hand press into mine, firmer. The slam I feel in my stomach rages with excitement. I don't want to break this moment. I take my fingers and snake them around hers, intertwining them. This feels like home.

I feel her breath on my cheek as she leans in closer. Her free hand comes down next to my shoulder. It's as if she's stabilizing her body, bringing her even closer still.

I take this as my sign and move in.

I lean in to kiss her as she suddenly thrusts herself backwards. She's on her haunches holding something in her hand and then she waves it in the air—her cell phone. "Sorry. I had to grab this. I dropped it when you pulled me down with you." She wipes off the screen with her shirt before she dials. "Good thing it didn't go in the ditch. Looks like that front tire is jacked now, so I'll call Maisey to come get us."

"Sounds good." I can only agree as I stand up and attempt to brush myself off. I'm covered in mud and about to give up, when she hangs up her phone, disappointed. "She's not answering. I'll text her and we'll see if she answers me."

I see this as a sign from the heavens. We're still in the ditch, but we're in it together, our bodies so close I feel the heat of her body. Freya giggles and shakes her head.

"This would happen to us, wouldn't it?" she says with a grin.

"Hundred percent." I grin back. "Sorry I took you down with me."

"There's no place else I'd rather be." The laughter now gone, she searches my eyes as she licks those full and luscious lips of hers. I groan inwardly as I try to pull my gaze away. Do I want this so badly that now I'm seeing things?

I go back to those kissable lips and, dragging my gaze up to meet hers, I'm stunned when I think I see—no. I know I see—she's staring at my lips, too.

This is happening.

I didn't think it would happen tonight. She just got back, and now here she is in front of me and I'm going to plant a kiss on those lips that will take her breath away. I'm going for it. I move in, just as she closes her eyes—

And that's when I hear the horn honk.

"Is that you, Wyatt Hogan?"

Spinning around, I see Dub, of all people, in his truck pulled over on the side of the road. He hangs out the driver's side window pointing to our bike carnage. "Looks like you guys need some help. Good thing I came along."

Chapter 5

"Oh, lucky for us!" I hope he can detect the sarcasm there.

I watch Freya hop up and accept his offer, taking away any chance I have to open the window a little more between us.

At least for tonight.

Chapter Six

Freya

"I think Wyatt tried to kiss me last night."

I'm whispering to Maisey as I squeeze my way past her behind the counter to refill the cutlery tray after the breakfast rush. "I'm not sure, but it felt like it was about to happen."

"What?" Maisey spins around so fast she almost takes down the red, white, and blue bunting draped on the counter with her wind speed. "Tell me more."

"There's nothing else to say. I think maybe, but I'm not positive. Things were a little—"

"Awkward? Weird? With you, I'm willing to bet awkward is how it went."

I smack Maisey in her arm before bending over to restock the forks. "I wasn't awkward. I was surprised, if it was what I thought it was. And, like the last time this happened, I don't think I handled it well."

I look up to find Maisey staring at me. "What do you mean?"

"Don't glare at me." I groan as I stand up, then fill her in on the bike jump and subsequent bike crash and burn that was last night. "When I was there looking down at him, I thought he was staring at my lips. He actually had a look that was smoldering. I finally understand what that word means. I was about to kiss him, but I saw my phone and..."

"You took the easy way out, didn't you?" Maisey shakes her head as I nod mine. "You are so immature."

"It's not immaturity." I glare at her. How dare she tell me the truth. Who does she think she is?

"You're right, it's fear. You're scared of falling for your best friend, aren't you?"

I don't want to hear it because Maisey is usually right. I'm contemplating this when I see the man of the hour walking up to the counter in his dress blues smiling at me.

"Hello, Fire Marshall Wyatt. Need a coffee?"

"I'm a fireman. Not a Marshall." He nods to Maisey who stands beside me. "Hey, Maisey."

"Hot lips." She nods curtly as he cocks his head to one side, cutting a look my way.

"What?"

"Nothing." I wave the comment away and push Maisey toward the coffee machine. "Can you make Wyatt a coffee?"

She wiggles her eyebrows at me as she points to the box on the shelf at my feet. "On it. Can you hand me a filter and some coffee beans? They're in that box there. For here, Wyatt, or do you want to take it to go?"

My head is buried in the box when I hear the lilt of another female's voice chime in, answering for him.

"He'll have it here, Maisey. He's joining our table."

I stand up, and fast, to find one of the most beautiful women I've ever seen in my life standing in front of me with her arm looped through Wyatt's. Her auburn hair is twisted back into a French braid, and her skin is porcelain perfection, dewy and fresh. She looks like she stepped off the pages of a magazine while I pretty much smell like crab cake sandwiches and look like a wet french fry.

When she sees me, her eyes light up. "Are you Freya?" She holds out her hand. "I'm Dylan. It's nice to meet you."

My jaw goes slack. "You're Dylan?"

"I think my dad wanted a boy, so he and Mom compromised on my name." She's still holding out her hand, which I finally limply take and pump a few times in hello. Satisfied, she turns her attention back to Wyatt. "I'll be at our table going over our plan for the raft race, then we're heading down to the starting line. Join us before you go?"

Wyatt nods, and I find myself wondering when he was going to tell me his good friend Dylan was a straight-up supermodel/angel who accidentally landed in Lake Lorelei. Who is this woman?

"Freya?" Broken from my thoughts, I realize Wonder Woman is looking at me. "Do you want to join us this morning?"

I look at the three faces looking back at me. "Join you for...?"

"Have you really already forgotten?" she asks in her most Southern drawl. "It's the Lake Lorelei Raft Race today, and all proceeds this year go to the local Alzheimer's charity."

That's right, my fogged up brain suddenly remembers Maisey talking about this my first night home. The raft race is an annual event with all of the local businesses racing homemade rafts on the lake. It happens during Fourth of July week celebrations every year. The proceeds from entry fees are donated to a local charity, and this year's charity is one that's obviously close to my heart and was chosen by Maisey, who sits on the board for the Lake Lorelei Business

Council. But, let's be clear—in no way do I want to end up on a raft in the race.

No. Way.

So why am I bobbing my head up and down like a stunned deer? "Oh, count me in, I'm definitely joining you guys. I can help set up, bring down some food. I'm great at cheering."

Dylan laughs, her brown eyes sparkling with what I deem as delight in seeing me squirm. "We need another person on the Red Bird raft. Maisey said you might want to do it, and if so, can you be there in an hour?" She winks at me while she hip checks Wyatt, who stands beside her biting back a laugh.

I turn to my aunt who surely won't want to let me go right now. "I think I'm needed here, but thank you."

"Oh no." Maisey crosses her arms in front of her chest as she puts me in her sights. "I need you on that raft more than I need you at the cafe right now. I over-scheduled servers today because of the holiday, so we'll be good without you."

Without even looking at him, I know Wyatt is secretly enjoying this moment. He knows I'm not a fan of the raft race and putting me in any kind of competition, well, things can get crazy depending on my mood.

But this *is* for charity.

And, to be completely honest, I'd be a madman if I let him walk away and spend any more time alone with that true-to-life goddess.

So I do what I need to do.

"Well, count me in! Let's go win a race."

* * *

41

Always be careful what you wish for. Always and in all ways.

I for one wish I had thought twice before agreeing to get on this splintered piece of broken wood that's barely being held together by the fraying rope that binds its planks. But seeing as I'm in the middle of the lake, and we're in first place thank you very much, it's simply too late now.

Our team representing the Red Bird consists of a few people—Dylan, Wyatt, Jack, and Reid are all from the fire-house. Reid is not only another fireman, but he's also the son of Pastor Michael and Pat Shannon, and apparently he, like everyone else at that stinking firehouse, is also a part-time Greek god. Where are they breeding these people?

There's also a girl who waits tables part time with us and her daughter named Nikita, a dishwasher named Carlos, and then there's me. Jack and Reid are on the front of the raft, using their strength to give us a good lead. Wyatt and Dylan are behind them, adding to it with their stamina which, while awesome to watch as they fluidly move in unison, is also nauseating because they look so good together. Carlos is paired with the part-timer at the back of the raft because of their power, leaving me partnered with an eleven-year-old girl in the middle.

I see how I rate.

My big mouth will one day be my downfall. I'm not really great at sports, and the idea of breaking a sweat in the humidity of a July afternoon in North Carolina is not in any way appealing to me. I'm ashamed to admit the only reason I wanted to be a part of this was because I was definitely feeling competitive, but it wasn't the race that had me so fired up.

I glare at Dylan's back in silence, but it's still deafening as far as I'm concerned. If looks could kill, I mean talk, mine would say "get off the raft," but never mind. I can't help but watch her move, she *is* balanced right in front of me. It doesn't help that she is ever so graceful and moves with perfect precision as she slices the water with her paddle— it's like she's cutting butter with a hot knife.

Now I'm not unfit, but I'm not the most fit human being. I would call my level of fitness normal, but when I look around at my raftmates it seems I'm the only one who is struggling, huffing and puffing and trying not to have a heart attack. Even Nikita beside me is focused and in her own world, her breathing steady and her gaze set on the finish line.

I hate this kid.

I dig in and take a huge gulp of air, feeling beads of perspiration trickling down the side of my face. I see Wyatt turn his head to sneak a glance back at me and throw a smile my way. Sweet guy, isn't he, wanting to make sure I'm not clutching my heart and dying as he wins the race. The smile seems to be full of pity, which makes me mad. I may be a hot mess right now, but I do not need pity. I grip the paddle in my hands harder and start chopping at the water like I'm holding a pickaxe. If we're going to win, I'm going to be an integral part of the team, dang it. I quickly find my groove and slide into a hypnotic rhythm with the team.

I'm paddling, like it's my job, when something in front of me flashes and Dylan cries out. Looking up, I watch in horror as Dylan's paddle comes sweeping up out of the water, and, in slow motion, I feel it slap against and connect with my chin. I feel the crack, and my hand flies to my face, expecting to feel a gap where my chin should be. I jump straight up, not thinking, holding my face and screaming in pain. I glance down to find Wyatt and Jack are both yelling at me.

"Sit down, Freya!"

"What are you—"

I never hear the rest of what they're saying. Next thing I know, I'm in the air, weightless, then falling head over heels into the water. Hitting the surface, I sink to the bottom, my feet hitting the soft mud that feels like quicksand but is probably just years of duck poop layered on top of itself forming the bottom of the lake. I almost gag underwater at the thought.

I sputter to the surface and take a giant gulp of air. My jaw throbs. Through my pain haze, I think Wyatt's throwing himself off of the raft, but I'm not sure. I'm swimming in the lake, but I'm swirling in my own embarrassment. My eyes close, the pain is too much. It makes my eyeballs feel like they may burst from their sockets.

In a matter of seconds, Wyatt and his amazing arms are wrapped around me. He threads himself behind me, pulling me on top of him as he slips into a backstroke and heads toward shore. When he gets us safely to the beach, in one graceful motion he manages to sweep me up with one arm to position me so he can carry me with both. Like a super-hero, only he's not wearing a cape. I glance down and realize I'm snuggled right up against Wyatt's chest, with my head cradled in the nook under his chin.

I don't want to leave this spot. Ever.

Unaware of my internal dialogue, Wyatt jogs to a picnic table and lays me down on top of it. I open one eye and squint at him, watching him grin as he leans over me.

"You're so dramatic." He winks, little drops of water spilling down from his face to his...oh wow. His chest. I must have been staring at it pretty hard because he gets this weird expression on his face. One of his hands crosses his stomach and covers his abdominal area, right around the

spot where the lines form a perfect V showing off his definition. "What are you looking at?"

You. "Nothing. Just getting back into focus." I clear my
throat as he looks around, flagging Reid before he turns his
attention back to me.

"I'll go get you some water, okay? Stay here."

My chin continues pounding with pain. "That won't be
a problem."

I watch as he runs over and joins a few other guys from
his fire station who are standing nearby on the scene. It's
incredible, they all look like he does in shorts—hot.
Honestly, if I didn't hurt so much, I'd get up and tease him.
They look like they're about to shoot a calendar for hot fire
daddy bods of the century. Considering the raft race is for
charity, with these guys around I feel like I've been dropped
into a magazine photoshoot.

The day has made me realize one thing, though, and
that is charity is *good*...in fact, I'm planning my own chari-
table contribution to the Lake Lorelei Fire Department this
year.

* * *

Once I get Wyatt to realize I don't need stitches (which
seems to be a thing with us), I finally convince him to take
me home. He wants to go to the hospital, but I want my bed,
so I get him to agree but only under the caveat that Maisey
would be there. I'm a clumsy human and I know when I
need surgery and when I need two aspirin and a good
night's sleep. Today, I'm writing myself a prescription for
the latter.

However, when we get back it turns out she isn't here. I
walk into the kitchen to find a note on the counter saying

she's staying late at the cafe to prepare for the rest of the week and would most likely stay in town at a friend's apartment that's close to the cafe. Can't blame her for doing that when a week is as busy as this one is for her. Makes it easier for her to open tomorrow at five in the morning if she only has a block to walk to work.

"I guess that means you get me as your nurse for the night." Wyatt stands before me, his arms crossed in front of his chest and his voice husky and low. "And you can't argue your way out of this one. As your friend, I wouldn't leave you here, and as a fireman who has sworn to protect and serve my community, I can't in good conscience leave you alone." He walks over, plunks himself down on the couch and throws his feet up on the coffee table. When I make eye contact with him, his eyes twinkle. "So, baby, I'm yours."

My head still hurts and so does my chin. I don't have the energy to argue, but I'm also not sure if I have the energy to fight off the feelings that are seriously bubbling to the surface right now. I want to shove this down and compartmentalize the situation, at least for a few days. The last thing I need while I'm trying to decide where to live is a complication. And stepping over this line with Wyatt could complicate things.

I sigh and look at the man sprawled across my couch with that lazy smile playing across those sexy, full lips of his. What is it Maisey likes to say? "If you can't beat 'em, join 'em."

I walk over to the couch and scoot in next to him. "Move over, I'm the one who was injured."

"Pffft." He nudges me with his elbow. "You'll have a mark, maybe some bruising, but we did get ice on it pretty quickly."

I groan. "All I need is a bruise showing up on my face. Maisey will never let me live it down."

Wyatt leans forward and swipes the remote from the coffee table. "Feel like streaming something?"

"I do." I reach over and grab the remote from his hand. "Again, as the injured, I reserve the right to choose. And tonight I pick Dirty Dancing."

"Good choice," he murmurs, thumping on a pillow which he's stuffed behind his head. "Are you going to treat me to a concert with every song tonight?"

"Ahhh, the good old days." It's true. I know every song and have made this man sit and listen to the album more times than he probably wants to admit. "Lucky for you my head hurts too much, but raincheck?"

I hit play on the remote, and Wyatt scoots down, making more room for me on the couch so I can lie down. He even helps me get comfortable by tucking a pillow under my head. "You good?"

"As much as I can be with a severe head injury."

He chuckles. "It's not severe, you big baby."

"It hurts like I was hit by a fuel tanker. Dylan's got a powerful arm." For all I know she did it on purpose.

"She feels terrible and wants me to tell you she's sorry. She insisted she come over and help me take care of you, but I told her not to."

For that I am grateful, but I have to ask Wyatt about her. I decide I'm going to try to sneak in a question like it ain't no big deal. "Tell her I said thank you, but all's fair during the raft race. Was this her first one?"

Wyatt nods. "She's only lived here a few months. Here, you lie down all the way, I don't want to hog the couch." He gets up and sits in the chair opposite me, and changes the subject, thus changing tactics. "Can I get you anything at all before we start the movie—food, aspirin?"

I shake my head no. "I'll be fine."

Wyatt sits back in his chair, and I sink deeper into the couch. It's not long before I'm sneaking looks his way while we watch the movie. I want to ask him if he was going to kiss me. Did he mean to do that or was I imagining things? I want to tell him I think I feel something, but there's a huge possibility he'll laugh at me.

Do I want to open this door or slam it shut?

My mind screams, *Get over yourself!* And it's not wrong. I'm an adult, this should be so much easier. The fact that I am a grown-up woman who has a mind of her own spurs me on. I'm going to tell him.

I'm going to tell him how I feel.

I am going to tell him how I feel and I am going to do it right now!!

I sit up, the television flickering its lights across the darkened room, and I stare at him. He turns to look at me, pointing to the TV and laughing at the scene where Jennifer Grey as Baby shows up to the party carrying a watermelon. Patrick Swayze asks why she's there, and her answer? "I carried a watermelon" and it's always cracked us up.

Wyatt starts to turn away, only he doesn't. His eyes meet mine and they lock.

This is my chance. Now or never. I can do this.

"Wyatt?"

"Yes?"

Can we try again? Would you try to kiss me one more time so I can react differently? "I have something I really want to say to you."

Chapter 6

He looks at me, his face clouding with concern. "Are you okay?"

"Yes I am. I—" *I want to tell you I've been thinking about you non-stop since I saw you the other day, but guess what? I've already talked myself out of it because I'm a chicken.* "I want to say thank you. For today."

He cocks his head to one side and looks at me weird, but that's par for the course with us. Crisis of the heart averted.

For now.

Chapter Seven

Freya

Sprawled out on a red-checkered picnic blanket, Wyatt rolls over dramatically and grabs my arm. "My stomach is going to implode. I'm having a Red Bird baby. Can you please call for help?"

I grin as a few of our picnic-blanket neighbors sitting around us shush Wyatt for speaking up so loudly. He catches my eye, and we both throw our hands to our mouths, stopping ourselves from laughing out loud and making the other folks here irritated. The past few days have kept us both busy, but we managed to find time to make a date for Lake Lorelei's Movie Night in the Park. After only an hour(?) together, my sides hurt from laughing.

The makeshift screen in front of us flashes with special effects from a scene in the movie we're watching. Like Wyatt noted, it's no Dirty Dancing, but it'll do. Thank goodness Maisey had enough forethought to hook me up with a picnic basket full of goodies for dinner as well. If the way to a man's heart was through his stomach, I was on the winning side of things with Wyatt tonight.

"Pass me another slice of pie, would ya?"

Chapter 7

I lean on my arm and push myself up so I'm sitting with legs crossed beside Wyatt, who is now holding out his hand in wait. We've both been occupied with our responsibilities; he's been at the fire station non-stop getting ready for the parade, giving tourists tours of the station, and helping the team with safety measures around the fireworks display. I think he even said he'd been wrangled into an extra shift, while I'd been held captive at Red Bird by Maisey, assisting her with the picnic baskets she made for movie night as well as pre-ordered July Fourth meals for tomorrow night's fireworks extravaganza. The woman gets up before five in the morning every day and goes to bed by ten every night—and I still can't understand how she gets it all done.

I want to say I've been so busy I've not even had a chance to think about Wyatt, but the reality is that he's all that's been on my mind. That, and where I'm going to live in a few months' time.

During my shift today, when I was restocking the sugar caddies, Maisey asked me again if I had thought more about moving home. I didn't want to get her hopes up, but I did tell her that I was still considering it because it's a strong possibility. When she asked if I would be coming back for me or Wyatt, I stopped what I was doing to stare at her, a little miffed.

"Do you think I would only move back here because of a guy?" I shoved a sugar packet in its place, a little too vigorously because the packet ripped open and sprayed sugar crystals all over the counter. "I'm capable of making a decision that's based on what I want to do, you know."

Maisey laughed at me. Not with me, because I wasn't laughing, but at me. She sat down at the counter in front of where I stood and took the caddy out of my hands.

"I'm not asking if you would be moving back for Wyatt,

I'm simply asking if you are. But I want you to know that if Wyatt is included in your reasons why, I think that's okay. More than okay, really."

I leveled my gaze at her. "Well, then, it's a strong yes that I'm coming back. As for where Wyatt fits and if he fits, I have no clue." I closed my eyes and rubbed my chin, which looked good from the makeup I had on it but still hurt. "I kinda realized over the last few days that I may really feel something for him, but I'm not sure because he's also really hot and a fireman, so maybe I'm just man-deprived after all of my failed relationships?"

Ooof. That came out all at once.

Maisey tilted her head to one side and swallowed a laugh. She reached out and grabbed my hand, shaking it vigorously. "Congratulations for finally realizing what you have right in front of you. One thing I can say in my experience is that when you find someone who hits you here"— she tapped her heart with the open palm—"you do what you can to not let them go. So, what's the plan with Wyatt?"

My stomach filled with butterflies. "The plan is...well— I guess we might..."

"Oh boy." Maisey rolled her eyes. "You're not good at this, are you?"

I shook my head from side to side as I continued to rub my temples. "Not really. But I'm also still injured from the raft race so that could be affecting me."

"Excuses." Maisey wagged a finger in my direction. "Food is the ultimate way to any man's heart, so let's start there. You going to movie night?"

"I am. With Wyatt." I nodded as I resumed restocking the caddies. "We're meeting at the park."

"Well, text him and let him know you'll have dinner sorted out." She stood up on her tiptoes and peered beyond me into the kitchen. "We've got plenty back there for me to whip up some gourmet sandwiches and a few side dishes, and of course a few slices of pie. I think the Book Club forgot to pick up their order, so it's yours."

"I'll take it. One man's trash is another man's treasure."

"My pies are not trash, so bite your tongue."

I had watched Maisey as she hopped up and proceeded to organize a basket, filling it to the brim with anything and everything we needed. Now, I'm sitting here in the middle of the park on a blanket with Wyatt, the basket almost empty except for a few slices of Book Club pie that's left over.

I reach into the basket and grab a slice of Poe's Pecan Pie (guess what author they're reading this month?) for myself. I've already had two pieces, but who's counting?

"Another slice, Freya?"

Wyatt's counting, that's who. "I don't need your judgement, especially after you've swallowed two pieces already yourself." I take my fork and dig into the slice, putting it all in my mouth and chewing it slowly. "Oh man. Heaven!"

I look down and find Wyatt gazing up at me with that lopsided grin of his. My heart skips an actual beat. How have I never noticed how sexy that smile is? I take a chunk out of the pie with my fork and hold it out to him. "Want a bite?"

His eyes meet mine as he stretches his neck up toward me, and I lower the fork so he can get a taste. As I lean over, I feel a shock of electric current run through my body when he takes that bite—because the whole time he never stops looking straight into my eyes. It's like he's reaching into my soul and I am here for it.

"Good?" Maisey's food seems to be doing the trick. Wyatt sits up and scoots closer to me on the blanket.

"It's the best pie I've ever tasted." He licks his lips before grinning my way. "And I've had some good pies over the years."

I start to retort, but the whipped cream on his top lip is distracting me. I point to his face. "You've got something...there."

His hand flies up to his mouth. "Where. Here?" He rubs just to the left of the whipped cream.

"No, I'll get it." I grab a napkin. Not thinking, I raise it to his lips and gently wipe it away. I feel him staring at me, and the warmth from his breath hits my cheek, causing my stomach to do somersaults yet again.

I finish my mission and settle into daydreaming about those lips. I sit back and look around the park, checking out the crowd and seeing many familiar faces. And my stomach sinks.

There, a few blankets over from us, is Dylan. Good old Dylan. Oh goody, she's waving. I raise a hand and wave back as she points to Wyatt, signaling she wants me to get his attention. So I do—I hit him in the ribs with the pointy tip of my elbow. It's a little too enthusiastic judging from the cry that escapes his lips.

"What was that for?" he hisses.

"Whoops, sorry." I play innocent. "Dyls wanted me to get your attention."

He looks at Dylan and waves but turns back to me in a flash. "You know, there's nothing going on there, Freya. Really. We did go on a few dates when she first came to town, actually two in total, but she's solidly in the friend zone."

Why is he telling me this? Do I reek of jealousy all of a sudden? I mean, I should because as much as I hate to admit it, I am feeling a touch of petty jealousy about this, and it irritates me because I feel like I have no right.

"I'm not worried about her." Okay, so I fibbed. I look back at Wyatt, who knows me better than that. He wags a finger at me, making me laugh. I swat him. "Be good. The movie's almost over."

He turns his attention back to the movie, but I'm still plotting. If Dylan is in the friend zone—yay—then one of us needs to make a move here. The one thing I keep coming back to over the last few days when I think of Wyatt, and why I'm feeling this way now, is that I'm the one who put us here—in the penalty box if you will. I friend-zoned us all those years ago, so it's only fitting it should be me to get us out, right? If the roles were reversed and the shoe was on the other foot, I'd be hesitant to try anything.

So, I lean over and do what any mature woman my age would do. I start a tickle fight. They always begin innocently enough. A poke here, a prod there, someone runs their fingers along your ribcage or gets ahold of your knee and then it's on. I make it as far as getting my fingers next to his ribcage before he figures out what I'm doing. Let me tell you...never try to trick a man who's been training for over a year to be a fireman, cause they'll win.

As my fingertips dance to their intended location, Wyatt's hand, which is lying in wait, snatches mine and he manages to flip me over so I'm on my back with him still beside me, but pinning me down with one arm. I can't believe one arm is that strong, so I sneak in a quick feel and cup his bicep for good measure, and oh, yes, he's that strong. The curve of his bicep in my hands is sculpted perfection indeed.

I pinch my lips together to keep from screaming with laughter as our very patient blanket neighbors once again shush us both. The music rises, signaling the movie is coming to an end, which means credits will be rolling soon.

Wyatt, who's on his knees, pins me down with one hand while his free one slowly creeps closer to that sweet spot on my side. The spot he knows is the most ticklish of all.

"Don't you dare," I hiss, but his eyes gleam—he's about to make contact. I prepare myself, ready to hold back more laughter, but when I look up at him, something changes. His features soften and the energy shifts. He isn't so much trying to tickle me anymore; he's still super close and he's not trying to go away either.

The butterflies in my stomach are about to pop.

"Wyatt! Didn't know you'd be here tonight. Hey, Freya, how are ya?"

Well, bless their hearts. We can thank Dub and a few other members of the fire department for the interruption of that magical moment. I really hope their timing is better when they have to put out a real fire.

Wyatt stands up to attention like a shot. "Hey, guys, didn't expect to see you here."

I stand up beside Wyatt, who walks a few steps away and is talking to Jack, while I say hello to Dub. "You guys here for the movie tonight?"

Dub nods, his silver hair shining as it reflects the lights in the park. "Jack was on call so we walked down for a bit. Fingers crossed it's a quiet couple of days. Holidays can get crazy and fireworks never help the situation."

"I bet. Will you be on hand with the safety crew for the fireworks display tomorrow?"

"Nah. I'll be there for a bit as an observer, but then I'm going to that party. Didn't Wyatt tell you?"

I shake my head, confused. "No. What are you talking about?"

"I thought Wyatt would have told you we're all going over to Dylan's for the fireworks tomorrow night. He's been helping her organize her party nonstop the last few days."

"What? No, Wyatt didn't tell me that was happening."

"Wyatt didn't tell you what?" Wyatt's chosen the perfect moment to walk up behind me.

I spin around, putting a hand on my hip. "That you've been planning a party with your friend Dyls the last few days?"

Wyatt's face clouds over as he crosses his arms across his chest, like he's closing himself off to me. "Did Dub tell you that?" He cuts his eyes at the burly, older fireman.

"Me?" Clearing his throat, Dub's hand flies to his chest, his index finger pointing to himself. "And...that's my cue to leave. See you guys later." Dub throws up a salute as he and Jack walk off, but I'm too busy and too focused to acknowledge either one of them.

"Yes, Dub told me, but that's not the point."

Wyatt rubs the side of his face. "I'm confused. Why are you calling her Dyls?"

"That's a red herring. We both know I'm calling her Dyls because it's not her name, it's my attempt at being acerbic. Were you going to invite me to go?" I can hear it: my voice cracks, threatening to reveal my feelings before I'm ready or have a plan for it. "You've told me how she's just a friend, but Dub said you've been busy the last few days helping her with this party. You also told me you've been busy the last few days at the firehouse...even going so far as to tell me you took an extra shift. What's going on?"

"Freya, I'd help any of my friends set up for a party. It's not a big deal." He shifts his weight from one foot to the other, which is his tell for when he's lying. Oh, Wyatt Hogan, I know you too well.

"You're not telling me the whole truth, Wyatt." It's my turn to cross my arms. "You didn't answer my question. Were you going to invite me to go with you to Dylan's tomorrow night?"

I watch and wait. He shifts weight again to the other side. He knows that I know and the look on his face tells me I'm right.

"No."

My stomach sinks with surprise and sadness. "No?"

"No, but I can explain why." He steps forward and reaches out for my hand, but I take a step back. Defensive habit, I guess, but I'm feeling a little let down. Honestly, between the sudden burst of feelings I've had for Wyatt and getting to the point where I enlist my aunt to help me win him over with food is a big—no, scratch that—*ginormous* leap for me. And, since I'm being honest, I'm feeling a little stupid that I got excited about the fact I might have a chance with Wyatt. Stupid may be too strong a word, but I'm definitely feeling more vulnerable right now than I did when we were having a tickle fight in the middle of a packed park a few moments before.

My, how things can change on a dime.

All of this leads me to one thought: I don't want to be here anymore. I want to go home, and I'm not even sure where home is at this point. Do I want to go to my apartment in New York or back to my grandmother's, where Maisey is?

And it hits me. I want to be where Wyatt is because that's home. But it seems like he doesn't feel the same way. So what do mature independent women like me do in times like this?

We. Retreat.

I bend over and start gathering up the empty plates and

cutlery strewn around the blanket, packing everything back into the basket. "I don't need to hear your reasoning, Wyatt. I think I'm just really tired and have had a lot on my mind the last few days, so I'm going to go home."

I can feel his eyes boring a hole in my back. "Freya, if you give me a chance, I can explain. I don't want you to be upset."

"I'm not upset, I'm disappointed." I stop what I'm doing long enough to face him. "I've been in the middle of a giant decision, weighing options and taking stock of the people I love and want to be around, and trying to figure out where I'm going to live. It's not as easy of a pick as I thought it would be. And being here—in Lake Lorelei, where I love to be—is making things more confusing. Just earlier today, I was thinking my choice was to stay—"

I stop myself from telling him. Telling Wyatt that I'm literally *thisclose* to moving back here.

"Stay here?" His voice sounds hopeful, or so I think. It could also be relief. Who knows.

"Yes. I mean no. Oh, I don't know." My hands fly to the top of my head, fingers twirling in my hair. I wanted to stuff my random thoughts back in if I could, but I can't. "I've got too much going on. I can't think straight, so I'm going." I grab the basket and my things and start to walk away.

"Freya, I don't want you to go."

I turn and find Wyatt standing close to me, so close I swear I can see emotion swirling in his eyes. "It's not about what you want right now. It's about me, and I'm working at the cafe tomorrow for July Fourth. It's going to be busy, so I'm going to go get some rest. You should, too, you also have a big day, and night, planned for tomorrow."

Okay, that last part was petty, but I couldn't stop it. It felt soooooo good to say.

Freya

I feel his eyes on me, still watching me as I start the trek back to my car. I'd managed to find a parking spot near the border of the park, and if I knew Wyatt, he would still be standing there keeping tabs on me, watching my every move as I walked to my car. He knows me well enough not to follow me, and for that I am thankful.

I don't want him to see my tears of frustration that have finally escaped and are making their way down my cheeks right now.

Chapter Eight

Wyatt

Was Freya going to tell me last night she was staying in town? I shake my head feeling bewildered—at least, I think that's the right description of how I feel. I drop the large cardboard box I'm carrying to the ground.

"Good thing those aren't fireworks," the voice behind me jokes. I turn around and find Dylan, AKA Dyls, grinning at me, holding her own box stuffed full of decorations and other accessories needed for my master plan. "Where does this go?"

I nod, indicating the patch of grass on the slope next to the dock. "Drop it there if you don't mind, then feel free to run if you want. I know you don't have a lot of time to help me with this. I appreciate all you've done so far. You've been a huge help these past few days."

"Oh, stop it." Dylan straightens her baseball cap so the brim gives her shade from the midday sun. "I've got plenty of time to help you set up before I have to get to the garage."

"Dub doesn't have you working today, does he?"

"Nah." She shakes her head from side to side as she

kneels down next to the box and starts unpacking its contents. "The garage is closed for the rest of the week, but Dad likes to look over the accounting ledgers each week and I like to keep him happy. Seems like I'm good at that, or at least better than you are, huh?"

I wince as my friend mocks me. "Did you just make fun of how I'm handling things with Freya?"

"You bet I am." She chuckles as she stands up and holds out a string of Christmas lights. "Will these work?"

"Sure will. Start draping them around the pilings on the dock if you don't mind. I'm going to run an extension cord from the house later, so we'll have plenty of power."

"Roger that."

How had I done this to myself? In my efforts to win over the girl of my dreams, I'd asked the wrong person for help. Not that Dylan is the wrong person; in fact, she's the absolute right person for this job today. She's also an excellent firefighter, and being Dub's daughter, she's got a strong will and a wicked sense of humor.

And yes, I have been spending a lot of time with Dylan the last few days, but it's because I need her assistance. Dylan is a woman and she's got style, two character traits that elude me. I need feminine energy if I'm going to pull off this surprise for Freya.

"So she has no idea you're doing any of this?" Dylan's back faces me, but I hear the laughter in her voice. Fair enough.

"She has no idea. Not one bit. In fact, I think I'm in the doghouse right now because your dad let it slip that I've been hanging out with you the last few days."

Dylan winces. "Ouch. So now she thinks we're"—she points to herself and then back at me—"together?"

I nod, then shake my head. "It's a yes and no situation. I

told her there was nothing going on, then Dub happened. And she clammed up." I didn't add that I'd sent her a text message earlier that was still unanswered. A first in the history of Wyatt and Freya.

"Would it help if I said something, like explaining to her we went out and it only took two dates for us to realize we're friends?"

"I told her all of this. But she's wary. I've known her for a long time, and she's dated some turds who've lied to her in the past. She's got post-traumatic dating disorder or something." I grab a string of lights and begin looping them on the last few pilings.

"I've seen you do some incredible things the last few months. You can carry your weight and then some, so based on that, I feel like you'd be great in a crisis situation—which this will escalate into if you don't set the record straight." She snaps her fingers at me and points to a giant trash bag stuffed with goods by my feet. "Now, pass me a few of those throw pillows in that bag."

"Thanks for the encouragement. And yes, that was meant to be sarcastic." I throw a couple of bright red and white pillows in her direction. "Who even has outdoor throw pillows?"

"I do, and this is why you've asked me to help you. Makes me glad I brought a few of my old party supplies with me when I moved from LA last year. Who would have thought it would come in handy for you when you need help with your love life?" She rolls her eyes as she steps back to survey the dock. It's still light out, so we don't have the full visual impact yet, but we both can see where my spark of an idea is finally starting to come together. Well, my idea with the help of Dylan's professional event planning skills.

Next to me, I hear a low whistle escape Dylan's lips. "Not to toot my own horn, but wow. This looks great."

I can't disagree; she's worked her magic and then some. Once it's dark, this spot is going to be exactly as I need it to be, and I can't wait to see the look on Freya's face.

Freya has always loved the Fourth of July. Since we were kids, we've spent the night of July fourth together and usually ended up here, on her grandma's dock, watching the fireworks light up the night sky. Summer has always been ours, and if I'm going to have any kind of chance to win her over and get her to see how much I care, it's going to be tonight.

Dylan grabs her bag and car keys. "Okay, I'm outta here. You good for tonight?"

I look around and survey the scene before me. I want this to be right. I *need* this to be right—I've waited this long to speak up, so I can't screw up in the home stretch.

I go down my list; decorations and ambiance pulled together by a real life event planner? Tick. Although, I'm sure I'll have to help Dylan with her Intro to Heat Transfer and Fire Measurements course, which is a small price to pay.

Food basket prepared by the best chef around? Tick. Thank you, Aunt Maisey. And I'm happy to repay the favor by checking the Red Bird for any would-be fire hazards. Again, it's a small price to pay for winning over Freya's heart.

Playlist ready to go with some mood music later? Tick. It hadn't taken me too long to organize a list of songs I know she likes. I even included some from Dirty Dancing because for some weird reason, I've decided that's our movie. I just hope Maisey will remember to turn on the speakers, and turn up the volume, at the right moment.

Chapter 8

Now, the rest of this night...is all up to me.

* * *

Freya

Coming home to watch the fireworks from our dock solo was not in my original action plan, but it's certainly fitting for my current mood. Even though I wasn't in a war, I feel defeated, and apparently defeat has a smell and I think it's seeping out of my pores.

I open the door and find a smiling aunt jamming out and dancing to Katy Perry's "Firework" in the kitchen. Yep, Aunt Maisey is right here letting her colors burst, and loudly. To be honest, I need to laugh. The bruise may be feeling better on my chin, but the bruise of my ego is another situation altogether. Behind Maisey, I see a buffet of bad choices spread out on the counter which include, but is not limited to, a bag of Grandma Utz's potato chips, onion dip, a giant bar of chocolate, and what looks like sundae fixings as well. Comfort foods abound.

One look at me and Maisey stops her concert for no one and turns down the music. The woman can read me like a book. She crosses her arms, squints her eyes, and looks at me in that all-knowing way only family members can do. "I know it was busy at the cafe today, but you're dragging those feet like someone burst your happiness balloon. What's going on?"

I pull out a stool at the counter and plant myself in the seat. "I made a decision about where I'm going to live, and I'm coming to terms with it."

Maisey's face clouds over. "Judging by the way you

look, I'm thinking I'm not going to want to know where you'll be moving to, because it won't be here. Will it?"

"Actually, I've decided I *am* coming home. I'm coming back to Lake Lorelei." I shrug my shoulders, leaning into the back of the stool and making myself comfortable. I can feel my shoulders release some of their tension, and it's glorious. "I wasn't positive I wanted to come home, or that I could, but none of that matters. I realize I need to be here. I could feel the pull of this place as soon as I walked in the house and even the first shift back with you. New York will always be there, but time with you and the rest of the family here, that's where I want to be right now."

I barely finish before Maisey swoops over, pulling me into her arms and jumping up and down. "Yay! Yay! Yay! Oh, Freya, you've made me so happy. You're going to live here with me, right? Say you will because I don't think I could have it any other way."

"I will." I laugh as I extract myself from her exuberant embrace. "At least for the first year, if that's okay? I'll pay you rent and my share of the running costs."

She waves a hand in the air. "We'll figure it out. I'm just thrilled our girl is coming home. So, now that's outta the way, can you tell me what else is going on?"

I can never keep anything from this woman. "It's Wyatt."

"Okay, what about him?"

I fill her in on the night before. "I messed up, and I don't have the ability to go back in time and fix a parameter I put on our friendship. I stuck us in the friend zone because I was scared to lose a friend. My best friend."

"I swear I don't see the problem here."

I grunt my displeasure. "The problem is me, Maisey. I played a game and lost."

"Sweetie, you didn't play any games. And you surely have not lost anything."

I wag a finger at her. "This is where you're wrong. I started to feel something this week. No, that's wrong. I've been sitting with the feelings for years, and I was finally ready—see definition for 'mature enough'—to acknowledge them this week. The problem is that I'm too late to the party and that boy, who you said had that crush on me oh-so-many-years ago, has moved on. I just needed to hear it so I can close this chapter, tucking it into the 'we really are just friends' basket and get back to normal programming." I take a sip of the iced tea she'd slid in front of me while I was talking. "I may have opened my heart to a possibility this week, one that isn't reciprocal, but it showed me it's time I started owning my choices. Which is a big reason I decided it's time to come back here."

Grinning, Maisey holds up her glass. "Then we need to toast to that. To making bold choices and owning them."

"Here, here." I raise my glass and clink hers, my grin spreading wider now that I've shared my choice with someone. Makes it real.

"Well, not to rush things here, but look at that." Maisey taps her watch. "Fireworks start in a few minutes. Feel like watching them on the dock?"

"Are you kidding? I'm already walking down there." I wink as I grab my drink and walk to the back door. "You coming?"

"In a few." Maisey nods her head in the direction of the stairs. "Let me run upstairs and grab us a blanket to sit on. You go on, I'll be down soon."

I start to walk to the porch door, but double back to shove a few potato chips in my mouth. I'm well aware I've now moved into "eating my emotions" territory and I don't care. Crunching away happily, I make my way outside and start down the pitch-black path to the dock.

As I approach the spot where the yard ends and the dock begins, there's a sudden flash of brightness as the world around me lights up—and it's not from fireworks.

In front of me, the old dock comes to life.

The path is lined with twinkling fairy lights snaking their way down to the dock. As I follow the walkway, I look up to see where lights have been strung on the posts, outlining the embankment and adding a romantic feel that I'm pretty sure this old baby has never seen before. On the decking, the part of the dock where we like to sit each year, someone has placed several small Mason jars full of flowers —white and blue hydrangeas and red roses, to be exact. I recognize the flowers from the bushes around the property. On the ground, delicate petals are sprinkled everywhere I look as if it has snowed red roses, and the effect is stunning.

In the middle of the deck area, a circle of lights border a decadent oasis: a large blanket has been spread and a bevy of pillows, both large and small, are strewn about. On the blanket sits a giant picnic basket with Wyatt standing next to it, grinning my way and holding his arms out wide.

My heart implodes.

"Ta da," he whispers, but only loud enough so I can hear him. There's that smile of his, lopsided, charming, and so, so sexy. I can't stop smiling, to the point I'm worried a firefly might get stuck in my teeth. Everything inside of me is jelly.

Wyatt holds out his hand, and I step closer, ready to close the gap on the slope between us, and I realize I'm shaking. As I take my first step toward him, instantaneously the first few notes of "Born in the USA" blare across the lawn.

And of course I jump—it startles me and I'm not expecting it.

Flinching, I feel my feet shift underneath me as the dirt moves, just enough that I'm thrown off-balance on the sloping hill. Losing the battle I'm waging with gravity, I land with a thud on the ground. Cue the domino effect as I begin an epic slow slide on my rear for the last five feet until the tips of my toes hit the wooden planks of the dock, stopping me.

"Freya!" Wyatt is right by my side. "Are you okay?"

"Nothing's broken, but my butt is going to be bruised for a very long time, just like my chin." I take his hand, letting him help me stand up. My bottom hurts too much to stay seated. Bruce Springsteen stops singing, thankfully. Not that I dislike Bruce, but I need my heart to chill out. "What are you doing here?"

"Where else should I be?" Wyatt takes both of my hands in his. "This is for you, Freya. I've been trying to find a way to show you how much you mean to me. I let you put us on the backburner ages ago—and against my better judgement, I might add. But when I look back and think about what it took for us to get here, I can only think it's supposed to be."

My heart is pounding, and I'm pretty sure Wyatt can hear it, it's so loud. I will it to quiet down. "You did all this for me?"

"You bet I did. This is why Dyls"—insert Wyatt's stern expression here—"has been helping me the last few days. We used the party as a diversion so no one would find out."

"So there's not a party at Dylan's tonight?"

"There is. But I wasn't helping her with it, I was getting her to help me do all of this." He tips his head, indicating in the direction of the picnic basket. "Well, Maisey had a hand, too."

Taking his hand, I step up on the dock and walk with him to the blanket. He bends over and begins to pull out an assortment of plates and treats from the basket.

"We've got food, drinks, and someone made sure that we have something sweet as well." He stands up and hands me a dish. "I think this should be to your liking?"

I look down. Strawberry pie. "You know the way to my heart, Wyatt Hogan." Holding the desert in my hands, I look around at the scene once more, my eyes filling with tears. "This is so nice, Wyatt. I think it's the nicest thing anyone has ever done for me."

"Well, I think you're the person I've always wanted to do nice things like this for. The only person I want to laugh with, and at...always."

The air around us fills with the opening strains to "The Time of My Life." Oh, well played, sir. If he's got Dirty Dancing on his playlist, he definitely brought in the big guns.

I giggle. Straight-up, silly schoolgirl style, but I'm okay with it. "I wanted to be the one who told you how I feel. I figured since I was the one who insisted we be friends, I should be the one to make the first move...so you don't slice open my cheek again."

"And take away the moment?"

"The moment?"

"The moment I get to look into your eyes and see your reaction...the moment when I tell you how much I love you. That moment."

Be still my heart. No really, be still, I'm about to go into cardiac arrest. Part of me thinks this is insane, how do two people fall this hard in such a brief window in time? I would think there may be some kind of passage to get from friends to here, a slower shift as we transition to more than friends—but the other part of me? That part knows we've been laying the groundwork to get to this very moment for years.

And I'm going to enjoy every moment from here forward. Starting right now. "You love me?"

"Of course I do. I have for a long time, and I decided the moment I saw you that this week I was going to make sure you knew this time." He runs his fingers through his hair. "I wasn't sure if you were going to be going back to New York or if you were really going to think about moving here, but it didn't matter. I wanted to make sure you knew that I love you. Wow. It feels great to say it out loud finally. I. Love. You, Freya Fredericks." He steps closer, taking my hand.

"Well, I love you, too, Wyatt Hogan."

"Can I finally kiss you now?"

"You'd better, cause I'm done waiting."

Wyatt lets go of my hand and then raises his, and I feel his fingertips comb through my hair. He cups the back of my head, tilting closer so our noses brush, his lips trailing their way along my jaw until they slant across mine.

Finally.

I close my eyes, Wyatt's lips press against mine, and I breathe him in. Sliding my hands up his chest, I let them snake their way around his neck, tugging him closer into my body. This kiss is better than I could ever have imagined. It's the kiss that says we're more than friends. It's a kiss that tips its hat to our history, but also steps back to allow our future. This kiss tastes like pink cotton candy, the sweetest lemonade from the county fair, and caramel covered apples all rolled up into one.

This kiss is the kiss I never knew I was waiting for.

Wyatt holds me close, the strength of his embrace safe and warm. I pull away and extract myself from our lip tangle, resting my cheek on his chest. He kisses the top of my head and nuzzles his way into the crook of my neck, kissing that sensitive part that trails from the back of my earlobe down the nape of my neck. Oh, this boy is going to be the death of me...and I'm happy to pick out the coffin.

Wyatt Hogan is mine. And I'm his.

He pulls back, still keeping me wrapped in his arms but craning his neck to look down at me. "So. Are we in this now for an adventure? For a meal?"

I open my mouth to answer, and a loud POP! sounds off. Startled, I step back, and another loud BANG! echoes on the lake and resounds across the water. Looking up to the sky above, I remember it is the Fourth of July. We're treated to the most magnificent and extravagant fireworks display I think I've ever seen. Of course, it could be because Wyatt just kissed me. I'll take it.

Wyatt stands behind me, pulling me close to him, and holds me against his chest so tightly I can feel the rise and fall from his breathing. I let my fingers dance along his fore-arms and caress his biceps. My imagination runs wild with the things I want to do to him, and I love it. I love him.

I turn my head and lean back, falling harder into Wyatt's body. I lift myself onto the very tips of my toes and press my lips close to his ear. "I'm in this for a lifetime."

Grinning from ear to ear, Wyatt turns me around so we're facing one another again. "Yeah? You sure about that, Fredericks?"

I place one hand on my hip and step back. "You don't think I'm being serious?" Wyatt raises an eyebrow, then steps away, stripping off his shirt. "Whoa, wait a minute. I mean, wow—" I stare at his chest. His lickable, glistening, ripped...

"Come on, Freya. Quit eyeballing me and get over here." Wyatt's still in his fire department issued shorts, striding to the end of the dock. "If you're in it for a lifetime, leap with me."

"I'm fully dressed!" The man can't be serious, but judging from the look on his face, he is.

It's the moment I know I've been waiting for and that our relationship has come to. Grinning, I stroll over to stand beside him, kicking off my shoes as I go. He reaches out a hand and his fingers find mine, threading themselves together as if they were meant to be.

I look down, staring at the velvet dark water that reflects the brilliant and dazzling display still firing off in the sky above us. That's some dark water. Pitch-black.

I can't see anything, but I do know one thing: with Wyatt by my side, it's going to be okay.

I look over at the man beside me. The man who was once a boy who lived here, in my hometown, and is my friend. My best friend. The person who I want my forever to be with. A warmth floods through me as I squeeze his hand and do the only thing that's right.

I leap.

Epilogue

Wyatt

While today was planned only with Freya in mind, I had to make sure we had a few other friends around to help me out. It's crazy to think that a few months ago I not only managed to finally get the girl, but to also help that girl move back home. In a matter of three days time, Freya's life in New York City had been packed up and we'd moved her back to Lake Lorelei and into the farmhouse with Maisey.

"Does Freya still think she's meeting you here for dinner?" Maisey asked as she walked out of the kitchen of the Red Bird. "And how are you doing? Ready for this?"

I didn't have to think twice before nodding. "I'm ready."

Maisey grinned. "Good, because there's about twenty five people on the back patio waiting to celebrate with you."

"Did Freya's parents make it?" They'd been gone for months traveling the United States in their RV, but had made a u-turn and headed home the day I called and asked them for permission to marry Freya. I know, a bit old fashioned, but hey...there's something super romantic about being old-school, you know? I was also hoping for bonus points with her dad, in a not-so-shameless way.

"They're on the patio with your parents and they are all giddy." Maisey chuckled. "I'm pretty sure Dub's entertaining them, too, so they'll be occupied listening to his stories about life as a career firefighter."

"He's got some great stories from his days when he worked in Los Angeles." I looked out the large window that faced the main street, hoping to spy Freya on her approach. "He's had some narrow escapes."

"I bet." I could feel Maisey staring at me, watching me pace back and forth. "I hope you're not trying to make one now?"

"No way." I stopped pacing and turned around, putting my hands on Maisey's shoulders. "I know with one hundred and fifty present certainty that I'm not ever going to make an escape from this woman. I don't want to."

"That's all I need to hear." She nodded in the direction of the back patio. "Come on, let's get the ring and then get everyone into position."

I followed Maisey out to the patio, which she and Dylan had painstakingly set up a bevy of all of Freya's favorite things: twinkling fairy lights strung overhead, little white candles in glass Mason jars placed everywhere—which screamed fire hazard to me, but thankfully we had half of the Lake Lorelei fire department here tonight—a grazing table that could feed the whole town and an assortment of pies; from caramel apple tart pie to chocolate peanut butter and including her absolute favorite...strawberry pie.

I spotted my grandmother standing with Freya's parents. I went to say hello and was pulled into a bear hug by Freya's father. Standing with them I found Jack and

Dub, who were flanked by Reid, Dylan and other members of our station. Even Pastor Shannon was there with his wife. My stomach did a little flip.

Nerves. Excitement. All of it.

It's getting real.

"I see that look on your face." My grandmother was suddenly beside me. A tiny lady, with a powerful energy around her and she's always been my rock. Putting an arm around her I pulled her in tight.

"I'm sure that look is me being confused?"

"It's excitement, perhaps laced with extra nervousness?" She tilted her head as she looked into my eyes, pressing a small box into my hand. "Wyatt, go get her."

I looked down at my hand to see what she had given me—my heart leapt. "Thank you. I love that this was your engagement ring and we get to keep it in the family."

"Same here. You know, I was blessed enough to have had one great love of my life with your grandfather. I've waited to hand this down to you for years, Wyatt. I'll be honest, I'm thrilled it's Freya who will be joining our family." She stepped back and looked around the deck, holding my hand tight. "Can you feel it?"

"Feel what?"

"All of the love hanging in the air for the two of you." She squeezed my hand. "We're all here to root for you, so you'd better get ready to seal the deal."

The fact my grandmother wanted me to 'seal the deal' was enough to not only crack me up but to also remind me I had gathered everyone here to be with me for my mission. I turned to the small crowd and waved, signaling for them to simmer down.

"Folks, I'll be back soon and then you can be as loud as you want to be. Until then, try to keep it down, will ya?"

Heading back inside, I could hear a few muffled cheers followed by a final warning SHUSH which came from Masiey, shutting the group up.

I paused at the door and looked around at this amazing group of people gathered here for us on this beautiful November evening. The patio sparkled and so did its occupants. The air had a slight chill, but it wasn't freezing cold yet so being outside was still enjoyable...as long as we kept those outdoor heaters on.

It was perfect.

I walked back into the Red Bird and stood at the counter, waiting for Freya to get here. Glancing at the clock on the wall, I knew it wasn't long. She'd be here any second.

Looking around the cafe again, I can't help but grin. It's filled with so many memories and the majority of them revolve around Freya. And I can't wait to make more memories with her and do it right here in Lake Lorelei.

"Wyatt?" The front door to the cafe opened and Freya stuck her head inside. "Are you here? There's a sign on the door that says the cafe's closed?"

The Red Bird was dark, but awash in moonlight. From where I stood, I was blocked by a shadow so she couldn't see me, but I had the perfect vantage point to see Freya as she glided across the room. My heart pounded in my chest.

I slipped out from behind the counter, walked up to her and wrapped my arms around her waist. "The sign says it's closed, because there's a special event going on here tonight."

"Oh." Her face fell as she stepped back. Her hands flew to her dress. "I wasn't aware there was something going on. Am I dressed appropriately?"

Now, I'm not any kind of expert but the dress Freya's

wearing is beautiful. It hugs her curves in all the right places and shows off her figure. "You're gorgeous."

"Really?" Smiling shyly, she twirled in a circle... and tripped over her own feet because, that's my girl. "Crap. It's the heels. Maisey insisted I buy them the other day to go with the dress. I didn't think this whole look was my thing—it's a wrap dress and I don't wear them usually. And it's been a while since I was this dressed up. You think it looks nice?"

"You could be in a brown paper bag, with holes in it, and I'd think you were better dressed than the Queen of England."

Her eyes narrowed playfully. "But could I wear it to the Met Gala?"

I nodded in agreement. "I have no idea what that is, but yes. You could wear it to the Met Gala."

She threw head back and laughed, then leaned in to kiss my cheek. "I'm starving. Are we eating here for this event or going somewhere else?"

"We'll be staying here, but before we eat I have something I really wanted to talk to you about first."

I took her hand and led her over to one of the tables, pulling out a chair for her to sit on. Slowly she took a seat, watching me intently and studying my every move. "Wyatt, what is going on?"

Reaching into the pocket of my pants, I pulled out the ring box. "I know that my life has always been leading me to this moment with you. The moment I get to do this."

I dropped to one knee. Taking the ring out of its box, I held it up in front of me as I looked into her eyes. "I don't want to do this thing they call life without you being a part of mine. You're my everything, Freya Fredericks, and you always have been. I know this is a new road for both of us, but I really hope you'll say yes and we can navigate it together. Will you marry me?"

Her jaw dropped. "Marry you?"

"Please?" I took one of her hands and held it in my free one. "If I promise to make sure we laugh every day and not go to bed angry?"

She nodded and leaned in closer to me, winking. "Do you promise to make the bed in the morning? And put the toilet seat down? That's a big ask, I know, but we need to nip any future arguments in the bud now."

"I think I can manage it." I tilted my head to the side. "Do you promise to not get mad at my work hours and the fact that some days I may come home smelling like smoke?"

Grinning, she cupped my face with her hands, pulling me even closer to her. "I do."

"I guess this is your way of telling me yes?" Taking the ring from its perch, I took her hand and slipped the ring on her finger. It was a perfect fit thanks to Maisey. She had managed to swipe one of Freya's rings she already had and gave it to my grandmother to have it matched for sizing.

These Lake Lorelei women. Brilliant, I'm telling you.

Freya nodded her head as she wiped tears from her eyes with the back of her hand. "Yes, Wyatt Hogan. One thousand times yes I would love to be your wife."

Standing up, I pulled her to her feet with me, wrapping my arms tightly around her waist as she pulled me into a kiss that took *my* breath away. Her lips on mine told me we were forever and I pressed back, letting her know I was hers and only hers.

As she stepped away, breaking the spell of our moment, Freya held up her hand admiring the sparkling bauble. "Oh, wow. This is gorgeous! I can't wait to show Maisey. And I need to call my parents. They'll want to know...and your grandmo...."

I held up my hand to stop her. "All taken care of, in fact," I pointed to the back patio doors, "if we go out there, you'll find the folks you mention and a lot of other people who love you very much waiting."

"What?"

"They're all here to celebrate with us." I threw my hands in the air. "Surprise?"

Her eyes sparkled. "Best surprise ever." She glanced at her hand and the ring. "Well, actually this is," she held up her hand, grinning.

"Ready to go out there and give them the good news?" I asked as I took her hand in mine.

Freya leaned in for one last kiss. "Let's do this."

***

Dear Wyatt,

Today was the best day of my life—I became Freya Hogan. I also made it down the aisle without falling, so I feel like we're already winning at marriage.

So, I'm your wife. How crazy is that? We're a family now and I couldn't be more excited. We made it through braces, stitches, bike races, retainers...all of the things! You've always been my perfect partner in crime, how lucky am I that I get to have my forever be with you?

I wanted to leave this note for you to find before we went on our honeymoon so you'd know a few things:

1. I love you so much my heart actually hurts sometimes. HURTS!! But in the best way possible.

2. I can't wait to start this new adventure with you...but

I meant it when I said you'll need to keep the toilet seat down.

3. I was thinking we should get a dog...and by thinking we should get a dog I mean I got a dog. For us. Maisey's watching him until we come back. He's a German Shepherd mix who needed to be rescued...Surprise?

4. Did I mention I love you so much it hurts?

5. And did I also mention I wanted to write you a letter because I was scared to tell you I got us a dog?

All of my love, now and forever...Freya x

***

Dear Freya,

I did find your note before we left. I decided to write you a letter in return, instead of, you know...talking to you since we're literally sitting right next to each other on the plane...but, I get it. We're playing a game...

Now that I'm your husband—how awesome is that!—I, too, have a few things I want you to know...

1. I love you more than anything in this world. When I said you were my everything, I meant it. That kind of love isn't going anywhere. Ever.

2. You are my wife and I get to tell everyone that I'm your husband! Do you even understand how exciting that is for me? Seriously. I will never take you or our marriage for granted.

3. So we got a dog? Awesome. I can't be mad. So you know, Maisey did text and say you were scared to tell me. She also told me about how Smokey (is that really going to be his name?) was part of a puppy mill. Of COURSE we're going to take him!!

4. Your heart is huge and I love you more and more each day.

5. No more dogs, though, okay? At least for now...we'll want some more once we have kids, though. ;) Smokey can be our practice baby.

Love you forever and ever...W.

******

Bonus Chapter

Freya

Spring has always been my favorite time of year. When I think of springtime, I can actually smell lilacs and hyacinths, two flowers that my mother always kept in abundance at this time of year in our home when I was growing up. Smelling these scents always takes me back to those easy days of being young, when everything was new and each day was an adventure.

Who am I kidding? I'm an adult, yet everything is still new—each day has been nothing but an adventure since Wyatt came back into my life. Wyatt...just thinking about him brings a grin to my face that is both sweet and silly, kinda like he is.

Sitting here now, on this perfect spring day on the patio outside of the home I share with my—ahem—husband, I'm surrounded by memories of our adventures so far. There's a metal garden sculpture in the corner he bought as a surprise when we got the house, and of course the hammock I got him for his birthday is strung up between two trees at the back of the yard. There's a giant wine barrel that Wyatt insisted we get on our honeymoon just because...and who am I to say no? I'm about to pinch myself when I hear a familiar voice call out.

"Freya? You here?"

"Outside, Maisey. On the patio."

Hearing my aunt's voice, I stand up and wait for her to join me. I spy her walking quickly through the kitchen, headed to the outside doorway to meet me.

"Are you alone?" She pauses at the door, looking over her shoulder, very conspiratorial, making me laugh out loud. "Has the rooster left the hen house?"

"Yes, you weirdo, we're alone." I close my computer and put my hands in the air. "And I'm not working at the moment so I can focus on our project." I looked down at Maisey's hands, which were empty. "You didn't forget it, did you?"

Maisey's jaw all but unhinged—I swear the bottom half of her mouth skimmed the patio floor. "Forget it? Me? No way! It's in the van. Let me go get it."

I follow her back inside the house, closing up the patio behind us, and watch as she jogs outside to her van and comes back quick as can be with a large white bakery box in her hands, showing off the Red Bird logo.

As she hands the package to me, I lean in for inspection. "Are you crying again, Maisey?"

"No." She sniffles, pulling a tissue out of her back pocket. "I'm not crying, you are."

My free hand flies to my cheek and sure enough, it's wet. "Ugh. These hormones."

"Wyatt's got nine months of you doing this, you know."

I bite down on my lip to keep from laughing, as poor Maisey keeps crying. "Nine months of me doing this or you? You know, I told you because I needed help surprising him with the news. You're going to scare him if he sees you, sobbing and blubbering, before I even have the chance to tell him."

"Good thing you're doing it tonight, then, huh?" She snatched the box back from my grasp and rolled her eyes. "I can't help it. These tears say I'm going to be a great godmother."

"I can't argue with that, just let me explain to Wyatt you've claimed the godmother honor, okay? I'm going to let him pick a godfather."

"That sounds so ominous." Maisey places the box on the table in front of us and opens the lid, revealing its contents. "Like we're in the mafia."

"Well, we're not, Maisey. We're in Lake Lorelei." I peer into the box at what looks like, from the outside, a giant cupcake with white icing. "So, inside that ginormous cupcake is the hint as to what the baby is?"

Maisey bobs her head up and down. "It's either pink or blue. I gave my assistant baker the paperwork from your doctor, so only Craig knows what you're having."

"You don't even know?"

Maisey shook her head. "Nope. I wanted that to be yours to tell me when you tell everyone else. I'm just glad we were your bakery of choice," she sang as she showed off her best curtsey, sweeping her arms to the floor for dramatic effect.

"Of all people, you know I wouldn't mind if you knew."

"I do know that, but I think I want to wait and have both of you tell me. More fun that way, cause I can keep crying." She throws me a wink as she indicates to the clock on the microwave. "It's almost time for dinner and I'll be needed back at work."

"Any special deliveries to the local fire chief tonight?" I

can't help but tease her about Jack McCoy, Wyatt's boss and the man my aunt has had a crush on for months now. Her and all of the ladies of Lake Lorelei, I might add. "Wyatt said you two spent a lot of time together at our wedding reception?"

My normally calm and cool aunt suddenly bristled like a porcupine who'd had an electrical shock. "There will not be any kind of special anything being delivered to Chief McCoy. Ever."

"Well, okay then." Since she actually snarled at me, I decided not to push it. And she called him Chief McCoy, not Jack. Oof. Not good. "Then I won't ask any more questions."

Maisey crossed her arms in front of her chest while vigorously shaking her head back and forth. Honestly, she looked like an irritated bobblehead doll. "Fine. Since you're pushing me to tell you..."

"Um—I'm not really pushing you, Maisey..." Oh, the drama was always strong with this one. But it's one of the main reasons I've always loved her to such epic proportions.

"...well, I'll only say this much; he asked me out, I waited for his follow up. He never called me to seal the deal and I have yet to receive an apology or a reason as to why he would do that. It's just so dang rude!" She lifted a shoulder and rolled her eyes. "So, that love affair is o-v-e-r."

"Forget him. He's missing out on one amazing woman." Walking around the table, I grab Maisey and pull her into a giant hug. I know her well enough to know she truly doesn't want to talk about Jack and the date that never happened, so I'm gonna let it lie. "Thank you so much for being in charge of this cake. It really means the world to me."

I feel her lips brush the crown of my head. "And you

mean the world to me. I told your mother when you were born I would always have your back, and I meant it. I love you so much, and I know a man who's going to be super excited when he gets home. He's going to flip out."

"I know." I laugh as I shake my head, touching my tummy at the same time. "A mini-me or mini-Wyatt. Crazy, isn't it?"

"Crazy fabulous. Gosh, what if it's twins? You know somewhere in our family we had fraternal twins...Eeeekk!!" As Maisey grabs her purse and throws it over her shoulder, I hear the sound of keys jingling in the front door.

Wyatt's home.

She turns to me, her eyes wild with excitement. "It's showtime. Have fun!"

As the side door closes, the front door opens.

I hear Wyatt's "Hey sweetie, I'm home!" right before I hear the clamour and crash which announces Smokey's arrival as well. Who would have thought a rescue pup like Smokey (half German Shepherd and half Labrador Retriever) would bring so much chaos but so much joy to our lives?

I kneel down to Smokey's level and brace myself as he rounds the corner, pivoting as he hits the turn on his right paw so he can launch himself in my direction.

Arms outstretched, I grab Smokey and wrestle with him, then give him a scratch behind his ears, making sure to kiss the end of his nose before standing up to greet Wyatt the same way.

"Hi handsome."

"And hello to you too, Mrs. Hogan." Laughter dances in this man's eyes, all the time, and it makes my insides get all gooey like a chocolate bar on a summer day. Wyatt pulls me into his arms and holds me close, nuzzling my hair as he kisses the top of my head. Ahhh, heaven. "I never want to take for granted coming home to you...but what's for dinner?"

Yep, my man likes to eat. "I've arranged for us to have a very special dinner tonight." Pulling away, I tilt my head toward the oven. "I've already made scalloped potatoes, there's a salad in the fridge and I'm going to put a few steaks—filet mignon, that is—on the grill for us."

"Wow." Wyatt's eyes light up as Smokey dances around us, bumping into our legs and wanting attention. "I must have done something right this week, huh?"

I decide to play coy, and start pulling plates out of cabinets and cutlery from the drawer for dinner. "I would say you've definitely done something that is very right, Wyatt. Very, very right actually."

I swear I can hear the gears turning in his head, trying to figure out what it is he's done that has warranted this meal. As I walk around the kitchen and start setting the table for dinner, both Wyatt and Smokey stay hot on my heels.

"Can you give me any hints?" Wyatt asks as he takes the cutlery out of my hands. "Maybe if I set the table you'll tell me?"

"Love how you're trying for bonus points." I swat at him, but let him take the cutlery and finish setting the table. "But, they're not necessary tonight. In fact we're doing things differently. Tonight, we're having dessert first."

There's a crash as Wyatt drops the remaining forks in his hand. "We are?"

Oh this man. "Not that kind of dessert." I roll my eyes and point to the Red Bird box on the counter. "That kind."

Wyatt eyes the box. "Did Maisey drop this off? I thought I saw her van here when I came home."

"I asked her to please make this especially for us so I could surprise you."

Wyatt crosses his arms and eyes me up one side and down the other. "Okay, this is very mysterious and also exciting. Tell me more."

Grinning, I open the box, pull out the giant cupcake, and gently place it on a dish. I slide the plate his way. "I need you to grab a knife and cut into this bad boy for me."

Wyatt narrows his eyes. "It's not a prank right? I'm not going to cut into this and like, some spring loaded fake snake is going to come out at me?"

"Where do you even get that idea from?" I push the plate his way again, trying not to laugh. "Just cut into the stinking cupcake and then I'll tell you."

We stand in silence for another few seconds. It's more like a standoff actually. I'm still trying not to laugh, and maybe scream with excitement, and he's worried I'm trying to prank him. What takes a few moments feels like years.

Finally, I can sense he's over it. He turns and grabs a knife off the table he just set and, turning back, he eyes me again as he slices into the cupcake. I watch as he expertly cuts a piece and starts to slide it out. Tears spring to my eyes, because I know we're about to find out something huge and I can't wait for him to know, too.

My husband. My best friend. The man who I get to start a family with.

I watch as he puts the piece of cake onto another plate and my tummy flips.

"Freya, why is the cake pink and blue?"

Well.

I wasn't expecting that.

"Because we're having twins." I'm trying really hard

right now to keep my voice calm, but the words escape me with a giant breathy whoosh. Twins. We're having twins.

Wyatt's head snaps up to attention and swivels in my direction. "Say what?"

"I'm pregnant Wyatt. You're going to be a dad."

I don't think for as long as I live that I will ever forget this very moment. The moment I get to see Wyatt's face as he finds out he's going to be a dad...to twins. Excitement, fear, amusement. So many emotions and all at once.

But—twins?!

Smokey leans against me, panting and his head swivelling to watch the both of us. I swear he had a smile on his sweet little doggie face like he was totally celebrating with us. Wyatt lets out a rush of air as he finally processes my news and rushes over to pick me up, spinning me around the kitchen as he whoops loudly.

I'm over the moon giddy as he places me, gently, back on my feet. "I'll be honest, this was supposed to be a surprise just for you but the universe got me, too. We're having two babies, Wyatt. Two!"

"Twins." Beaming, he shakes his head. "It's a case of the more the merrier, I say."

"But..twins!" I'm still processing, but Wyatt? He's my rock.

"Yes, but it's us, Freya. You, me, and Smokey—and we've got this."

Looking around at the home we've built together, and at this man in front of me who has been there all of my life— for good, for bad, and for some of the in between—I know deep in my heart he's right.

I open a drawer and pull out two forks, handing one to Wyatt. I dig into the oversized cupcake and get a big piece on my fork for myself. A swirl of blue and pink greets me and all I can hear are his words.

Yeah.

We've got this.

***

Don't miss When Sparks Fly…
Maisey and Jack's story is coming June 2022!

Acknowledgments

When I started publishing, I was told by several people that it takes a village to get a book out...and they were right!

I want to say THANK YOU to the amazing community I've found on Booktok. You guys are the BEST book buddies a girl could ever find!

A very special thank you to Cassie Brewton and her amazing daughter Lorelei who were so generous as to share the name with me for my fictional lakeside town, Lake Lorelei. I also want to thank Ana Ecaterina Luchian for suggesting the name of Freya for our leading lady.

Special VIP thanks to my poor cousin Shelly who has had to read several iterations of this story until I got it right. Girl. You are patient! Love you.

To my Beta Readers and ARC team...you are the superheroes not wearing capes, my friends. Thank you for your feedback and support! When I say I'm proud you're in my village, I mean it. You are ROCKSTARS.

Last, thank you to my amazing author community locally, virtually, and internationally. Your advice, insight, knowledge, help, and kind words are like sprinkles on top of a sweet sundae surprise! You're the bestest ever.

And THANK YOU if you're reading this. You're supporting an indie author, someone who loves writing and loves sharing stories.

I hope you enjoyed Sweet Summer Nights!

Happy reading,
Anne xx

About the Author

Anne Kemp is a bestselling author of romantic comedies. She loves reading (and she does it ridiculously fast, too!), gluten-free baking (because everyone needs a hobby that makes them crazy), and finding time to binge-watch her favorite shows.

Anne grew up in Maryland but made Los Angeles her home until she encountered her own real-life meet-cute at a friend's wedding where she ended up married to one of the groomsmen. For real.

Anne now lives on the Kapiti Coast in New Zealand, and even though she was married at Mt. Doom, no...she doesn't have a Hobbit. However, she and her husband do have a terrier named George Clooney and when she's not writing, she's usually with them taking a long walk on the river by their home.

You can find Anne on her website - come say hi! She'd love to hear from you: www.annekemp.com

Other Books by Anne Kemp

Stay up-to-date on new releases and special promotions when you sign up for

Anne's newsletter: http://eepurl.com/cCEKUT

Love in Lake Lorelei Series

Sweet RomComs sizzling with chemistry and bringing you all the feels. Set in North Carolina.

Get to know the locals and, most importantly, the

Lake Lorelei Fire Department!

Sweet Summer Nights (Book 1)

Freya and Wyatt's story is out now!

When Sparks Fly (Book 2)

Maisey and Jack's story is coming June 2022!

The Sweet Spot:part of the Fall into Love Boxset

The Sweet Spot is a novella in the Love in Lake Lorelei Series and will release as part of a very special boxset, Fall into Love. *This limited edition collection of romantic comedies is written by USA TODAY bestselling authors and up-and-coming comedy queens.*

Preorder now for May 1, 2022!

The Abby George Series

ChickLit with sass

(Sweet with heat: some swearing, closed door romance)

Rum Punch Regrets

Gotta Go To Come Back

Sugar City Secrets

Caribbean Romance Novellas

Part of the Abby George world but can be read as a stand alone

The Reality of Romance

Second Chance for Christmas

Thank you for reading!

*Thank you for reading Freya and Wyatt's story.
If you enjoyed this book, please leave a review. Reviews help authors and readers, and are vital to the success of every book.*

You can leave a review or follow me on Bookbub, Goodreads, or Amazon.

Happy reading!

You can always find Anne and her books at
www.annekemp.com

CPSIA information can be obtained
at www.ICGtesting.com
Printed in the USA
BVHW041020010223
657615BV00002B/91